KILLER WHALE

KILLER WHALE

Justin D'Ath

A & C Black • London

For Stella

Reprinted 2011
First published in the UK in 2011
by A & C Black
Bloomsbury Publishing Plc
50 Bedford Square
London
WC1B 3DP

www.acblack.com

First published in Australia by
Penguin Group (Australia)
A division of Pearson Australia Group Pty Ltd

Text copyright © 2008 Justin D'Ath

The right of Justin D'Ath to be identified as the
author of this work has been asserted by him in accordance
with the Copyrights, Designs and Patents Act 1988.

ISBN 978-1-4081-2646-2

A CIP catalogue for this book is available from the British Library.

This book is produced using paper that is made from wood
grown in managed, sustainable forests. It is natural, renewable and
recyclable. The logging and manufacturing processes conform to the
environmental regulations of the country of origin.

Printed and bound in Great Britain
by CPI Group (UK) Ltd, Croydon, CR0 4YY

1
MAYDAY!

'There's one,' squawked Harry.

'Where?' Dad's voice crackled in our headsets. He was sitting up front with the pilot and couldn't see which way Harry was looking.

'Over there!' Harry tapped the side window with his Game Boy.

'On the left,' I said into my headset-mike, leaning across my little brother for a better view. 'Between those two big icebergs in the middle of the bay.'

Ross Willis, our pilot, banked the Cessna 180 ski plane steeply to the left.

'Thar she blows!' he said. 'Nice work, Harry.'

We had been searching for whales along the Antarctic coast for over an hour and were nearly at the point where we'd have to turn back.

'Looks like a fin whale,' Ross said as we drew nearer.

'It's massive!' I gasped.

'They can weigh up to 70 tonnes. Only blue whales grow bigger.'

Dad was busily changing camera lenses. 'Are they endangered?'

'They were nearly wiped out before the International Whaling Commission banned fin whale hunting in 1976. Now only the Japanese go after them,' Ross said.

He dipped one wing to give us a better view of the huge mammal. It looked as big as a container ship in the middle of the wide, ice-flanked bay. 'Would anyone like to go down for a closer look?'

'You betcha,' said Harry, without raising his eyes from his Game Boy.

We flew round in a big semicircle over a fleet of monstrous icebergs and went buzzing back towards the whale in a long, slow descent.

Then the buzzing stopped.

We were all wearing headsets, which blocked out most of the noise. But not all of it – I could no longer hear the Cessna's engine. There was only the rush of air across its windshield, wings and fuselage. Dad and Harry were too busy gawking at the whale and the Game Boy to notice. But I was watching Ross through the gap between the seats. He'd suddenly become very busy checking dials, pushing buttons and flicking switches.

'Listen up, guys,' he said in a loud, serious voice. 'We might have a problem. Make sure your seatbelts are tight, and put your cameras and any other loose objects away where they can't fly about.'

Then he switched to an outside channel.

'Mayday Mayday Mayday! This is Zulu Kilo Victor November Mike, transmitting blind. Our engine has failed, we're going to be landing on or near the coast at approximately 130 degrees east . . .'

Harry looked up from his Game Boy. 'Who's May Day, Mr Willis?'

'Keep quiet, Harry!' snapped Dad, sounding tense. 'Don't bother Mr Willis now.'

While Ross repeated his Mayday call, I helped Harry

tighten his seatbelt. My hands were shaking so badly he probably could have done it better without me.

We're going to crash! screamed a little voice in my head.

I tried to ignore it. 'Put your Game Boy in the seat pocket, Harry.'

'But I'm nearly at a new record.'

'Put it *away*! Didn't you hear what Mr Willis – '

'Pay attention, guys,' Ross interrupted. 'The engine has lost power so I'm going to put us down on the ice. It shouldn't be a problem, but if anything happens you'll find a first-aid kit, life jackets and other survival gear behind the back seat. There's a fire extinguisher under my seat, and an axe on the floor in the front.'

'Wicked!' said Harry.

Sometimes it's embarrassing having five-year-old brothers. I should know. I've got two. The other one, Harry's twin, Jordan, had to stay home with Mum in Australia because of his asthma. I wished I was there, too. I wished Dad had never bought tickets in the World Conservation Society raffle, with a family trip to Antarctica as first prize.

An engine failure and forced landing were *not* part of the deal.

Nor was drowning or dying of hypothermia, which would almost certainly be our fate if we landed in the ice-flecked sea.

We were still a long way from shore. Ross had set a course directly into the bay, coaxing the ailing Cessna towards a wide, snow-covered plateau nestled between two craggy mountains. It looked like an ideal place to land. But without power we were barely moving. And we'd lost a lot of altitude. We still had roughly a kilometre to go when suddenly the Cessna began to pitch and shudder and jolt.

'What's happening?' I gasped.

'It's called a katabatic wind,' said Ross, struggling with the controls. 'You often run into them below 500 metres. A bit of a problem for us because they blow offshore.'

'*WE'RE GOING BACKWARDS!*' Harry shouted above the increasing howl of the wind.

I looked out the side window. He was right. We were being blown out of the bay. Out into the frozen wastes of the Southern Ocean. The next stretch of land was

Tasmania, nearly 3,000 kilometres north.

Even with a tailwind, a Cessna 180 can't fly more than 1,200 kilometres before it runs out of fuel. And that's with a full tank to begin with. Ours was half empty.

We were all going to die.

'I'll try something else,' said Ross, craning his neck for a view of the peninsula at the western end of the bay. 'Hold onto your seats, guys – things might get bumpy.'

He wasn't kidding. As soon as Ross kicked the rudder pedal, the Cessna flipped sideways, did a kind of cartwheel, then dropped like a stone. It felt like a rollercoaster ride, only ten times more scary. The sea rushed towards us. I closed my eyes and waited for the splintering impact that would smash the flimsy ski plane – and all of us in it – to smithereens.

It didn't happen. The falling sensation stopped. My seatbelt no longer cut into me. We seemed to be level. I opened my eyes. The Cessna was skimming across the water, barely three metres above the whitecaps. Heading directly towards the peninsula, a vertical wall of rock and ice that grew steadily larger, larger, LARGER . . .

Shishkebab! We were going to smash straight into it!

At the very last moment, Ross tipped the Cessna to the right. Its starboard wing nearly scraped on the ice. Yes, *ice*! We were no longer flying over water. Below us, a narrow shelf of sea ice stretched along the bottom of the cliff face. With a flick of the controls, Ross set the skis down. The Cessna went skidding along the shelf in a long hissing slide. A line of penguins saw us coming and dived into the sea. We finally came to rest less than a plane's length from the end of the peninsula, where the ice shelf met the sea in a turbulent boil of foam, broken chunks of icebergs and grey, crashing waves.

Slowly I unclenched my sweaty hands, leaned back in my seat and let out my breath. We'd made it.

BANG!

The Cessna jolted.

'What was that?' asked Dad.

Ross's voice was loud in my headset. And for the first time that day, he sounded scared. 'The ice shelf is breaking up,' he cried. 'Quickly, everybody out!'

2
CAPTAIN
AMAZING

Cessna seatbelts are more complicated than the ones in cars. There are lots of straps and buckles. But it's surprising how quickly you can get them undone in an emergency.

This was an emergency.

BANG! BANG! BANG!

It sounded like someone was shooting at us.

It felt like it, too. With every ear-splitting bang, the ski plane shuddered as if bullets were smacking into its fuselage.

Ross was first out. He dragged Harry's door open and helped him down onto the ice. Dad and I tumbled out on our side. The freezing katabatic wind bit at the exposed skin on my cheeks and nose. I was glad the rest of me was protected by multiple layers of wool, thermal cotton and Gore-Tex.

BANG!

A long jagged crack appeared directly under my feet. I grabbed the wing strut to take my weight off the ice. The crack split open and I found myself dangling over a zigzag of inky-blue seawater. My heart hammered, my legs scissored in the gusting wind. One wrong move, one slip of my hands, and I'd fall in. I remembered Ross's warning from earlier that day: 'It only takes two minutes in the Antarctic sea and you'll die of hypothermia.'

Slowly, glove over glove, I worked my way up the strut and along the wing until I was no longer over the deadly water. Then I gingerly set my feet down on the ice.

Harry and Ross came slipping and sliding around the nose of the ski plane.

'Where's Dad?'

Uh oh. I hadn't given him a thought since the ice gave way under us. 'He's right . . .'

The words died in my mouth. Where I'd last seen our

father, the fingers of two orange gloves clung to the edge of the zigzag gap.

'*DAD!*' Harry and I both yelled together.

Ross got there first. He lay flat on his stomach and dragged our father up onto the ice. Dad's face was as white as our surroundings and his weatherproof exposure suit was dripping wet from the chest down.

'Did the water get into your clothes?' asked Ross.

Dad shook his head. His breath made white clouds that whirled away on the wind. 'N-n-not t-t-totally. My s-s-suit k-kept m-m-most of it out.'

I didn't know whether it was the cold or the shock that was making Dad stutter. He seemed unsteady on his feet. Ross put an arm around our father's waist and turned to me and Harry.

'Get over to the cliff face, guys. I'll bring your dad.'

BANG!

A crack opened under the Cessna and one of its skis fell through. The plane tipped sideways. Its right wing smacked onto the ice, missing Harry and me by millimetres.

'*GO, GO, GO!*' Ross yelled at us across the sloping wing.

Grabbing Harry's hand, I ducked around the Cessna's tail and led him sliding and stumbling across the ice towards the tumble of snow and rocks at the base of the cliff. Out of the corner of my eye, I saw Ross and Dad appear around the other end of the ski plane, taking a parallel course to ours.

BANG! BANG! BANG!

A spider web of huge cracks shot out from under the Cessna. One raced straight towards Harry and me like a blue bolt of lightning. A gaping fissure yawned open at our feet. My boots slid crazily as I pulled Harry backwards. There was a loud creaking noise and a shadow fell over us. I flung a panicked look over my shoulder. The Cessna had fallen nose-first through the ice. Its tail stuck straight up, towering like a massive tombstone against the cloud-streaked sky. For a moment, it balanced there, rocking gently from side to side, then the doomed ski plane slid slowly down through the ice and disappeared.

'I left my Game Boy inside!' wailed Harry.

As if that mattered. Survival was the only thing on *my* mind. All around us, what remained of our icy platform was disintegrating in a volley of explosive detonations that sent clouds of ice crystals swirling away on the wind. The shelf creaked and rumbled and rocked up and down like the deck of a ship. I dragged Harry from one swaying ice floe to the next in a mad race to escape the maze of zigzagging cracks that seemed to follow our every footstep. They were gaining on us, getting closer by the second. I tried to run faster but it was impossible – our bulky thermal suits made us as slow as astronauts.

'SAM! HARRY!'

Dad and Ross had made it to the base of the cliff. Safe on the rocks, they were frantically beckoning at us to come in their direction.

'GET ONTO SOLID GROUND!' yelled Ross.

If only it was that easy. The gaps between the sections of ice were getting bigger every moment. Combined with the wind and the seesawing motion of the sea, it was becoming increasingly hard to balance. Halfway to shore, we came to a gap over a metre wide.

I slithered to a halt. 'It's too far for you to jump.'

'I'll use my super powers,' said Harry.

Harry plays a game where he's a superhero called Captain Amazing. Sometimes I wonder if it's just a game.

He seems to believe he really *is* Captain Amazing. Before I could stop him, Harry took a short run up and jumped.

Heart in my mouth, I watched my little brother fly across the gap between the two ice floes. It was a long jump for a five-year-old, but when Harry plays Captain Amazing he seems to get away with stunts that would defeat someone twice his age.

Captain Amazing made it across the gap. But only just. His left boot landed solidly on the ice, but the toe of his right boot caught on the edge of the floe and slid backwards – off the ice and down towards the glassy blue water 20 centimetres below.

Where something was waiting.

3
THE CREATURE FROM THE DEEP

The sea leopard (or leopard seal) is the most dangerous seal in the world. It's the only seal that preys on its own kind. And the only one that preys on humans.

But mostly it eats penguins. The sea leopard lies in wait under the ice until a penguin dives into the water. Then it strikes.

This one must have been hunting the penguins that were scared into the sea as the Cessna landed. When Dad fell through the ice, it probably saw his thrashing legs and came to investigate. Luckily Ross pulled him out in time.

But when Harry slipped, the sea leopard was ready.

The water between the slabs of ice was crystal clear. I saw the sea leopard when it was still four or five metres below the surface. At first sight I didn't know what it was. It looked like something from a horror movie, like *Godzilla* or *The Creature from the Deep*. And it was coming for Harry.

'LOOK OUT!' I screamed.

And jumped.

Sea leopards are huge. They can grow to more than three metres in length and weigh half a tonne. They don't have any natural predators except killer whales.

So they don't expect to be attacked by some puny little creature on the ice.

It wasn't my plan to attack the sea leopard. My intention was to jump across the gap and drag Harry away from the edge before it latched onto his foot. But the sea leopard got in the way. It burst out of the water just as I took off. I found myself flying towards it on a collision course. There was only one thing to do. Leaning my body back, I straightened my leading leg and delivered an improvised flying side-kick to the back of its ugly, bullet-shaped head.

WHAP!

The giant seal was taken by surprise. I wasn't big enough or heavy enough to hurt it, but the blow drove its wide-open jaws into the side of the ice floe, exactly where Harry's foot would have been if I hadn't yelled a warning. Instead of getting a mouthful of Harry, the sea leopard got a mouthful of ice. My knee buckled and I came down on the animal's wide, slippery neck, pushing it back down into the sea as I face-planted onto the ice next to Harry.

'Check out the humungous seal!' he said, peering into the water where the creature had disappeared.

I sat up on the small, wobbly floe, spitting out ice, and grabbed the back of Harry's full-body suit. 'Keep away from the edge. It might come – '

'*LOOK OUT BEHIND!*' Ross's voice cut through the whistling wind.

I looked round just in time to see a big slimy head squeeze up through the gap on the other side of the floe. It was only three metres away. I could see the dark, leopard-like spots on the killer seal's throat. I could hear its snorting breath. The sea leopard got its flippers onto the ice, then began to heave its massive, rubbery body up through the narrow gap like toothpaste oozing out of a tube.

Its weight caused the floe to tip, lifting our side up at a steep angle. Harry and I started sliding down the slope on our backsides. Straight towards the sea leopard.

We clawed at the floe with our gloves, but it was too slippery. Centimetre by centimetre, we slid down the ice. The sea leopard opened its oversized mouth and seemed to smile. Its body might have looked like rubber, but there was nothing rubbery about those long, nail-like teeth.

'Stand up,' I hissed, struggling to my feet and dragging Harry upright, too. Our gloves had no grip on the ice, but our snow boots had rubber cleats on the soles. They stopped our slide.

When we stood up, the sea leopard raised its head, neck and shoulders. Its honey-coloured eyes were nearly level with ours. They had a hungry look. Less than two metres separated us. Holding hands, Harry and I started backing away from it, taking tiny steps so we wouldn't slip on the tilting ice. One slip and we'd be toast.

Without warning, the huge predator flung itself forward.

Seals are lightning fast underwater, but on land they're out of their natural element. It takes a lot of energy to move all that blubber. And if you weigh half a tonne, you've got to move cautiously on ice floes.

The sea leopard lunged forward a second time, crossing the centre point of the floe. Suddenly our side of the 'seesaw' was heavier. The ice tipped down and our ungainly attacker fell flat on its face.

Harry and I jumped for our lives. Onto the next ice floe, then the next one, then the one after that.

I heard a splash and looked over my shoulder. The sea leopard had disappeared. It was back in the water. Harry and I stopped in the middle of a small, wobbling floe. Our eyes searched the rippling avenues of water that crisscrossed the broken ice shelf all around us. The miniature icebergs rocked gently on the waves. Every now and then, two would bump together with a loud clunk.

But there was no sign of the sea leopard.

'Where is it?' whispered Harry.

'I don't know,' I said, also whispering.

It was somewhere under the ice, looking up at us from the aqua-blue depths. Planning its next attack.

'Let's get onto that big piece of ice over there,' I pointed.

Holding hands for safety, Harry and I hopped from one floe to the next until we'd made it to the big one. It was roughly the size of a tennis court, but instead of service lines it was covered with fine blue cracks. Huddled in the middle of it, we felt reasonably safe.

'*Sam . . . arry . . . ide!*'

Ross was yelling at us again. His voice sounded faint. The wind made it impossible to hear what he was saying. Something about the tide? He and Dad were dwarfed by the massive icy escarpment that towered over them. And dwarfed by distance. How did they get to be so far away?

Suddenly I realised what Ross was trying to tell us. We'd gone in the wrong direction. Away from the peninsula, instead of towards it. We were 200 metres offshore. If we didn't get back in a hurry, the wind and the outgoing tide would carry us off into the Southern Ocean.

We'd be lost forever.

4
JAWS

'Harry, we've got to get to shore!' I cried.

But we got no further than the edge of our ice floe. In the two minutes since we'd arrived, the gap between it and the next one had stretched from half a metre to five.

Not even Captain Amazing could jump five metres.

We were stranded.

'Check out all the fish,' said Harry.

Deep below the surface, a wave of small, streamlined shapes went sweeping past our ice floe. They had long pointy fins and seemed almost to be flying underwater. That's how I recognised them.

'They're not fish,' I said. 'They're penguins.'

Suddenly, a dark shadow shot up out of the depths. The penguins scattered in all directions. But most of them disappeared under our ice floe, with the shadow in hot pursuit.

'It's the mean seal,' Harry said. 'Will it eat the penguins?'

'It probably won't catch them,' I replied. But I was pretty sure it would. The sea leopard wasn't fooling around. One or more of those penguins was about to become dead meat.

Better them than us, I thought.

'Yikes!' said Harry, grabbing my arm.

I turned and saw a sight that sent a tingle down my spine. The sea leopard was hauling itself out of the sea on the other side of our ice floe. It must have given up on the speedy penguins in favour of slower prey – Harry and me.

This time there were no nearby floes to escape to. The closest one was six metres away. The gap was growing wider every moment. Swimming for it wasn't an option. The freezing Antarctic water would kill us just as surely as the sea leopard.

The big grey seal came lumbering towards us, making the ice tremble under our feet. With nowhere to retreat, Harry and I skirted around the edge of the floe, trying to keep as much distance as possible between us and the sea leopard. The sea leopard didn't follow us. It kept going in a straight line until it reached the very middle of the floe, where it stopped and peered back over its shoulder. Not at Harry and me, but at the sea behind it.

I could swear it looked nervous.

Then something *really* weird happened. A penguin came catapulting out of the sea and landed nimbly on the edge of the ice. It was followed by another, and another, and another. Then a whole bunch of them burst out of the water simultaneously. They kept coming, until the edge of the ice floe was crowded with small black-and-white penguins. There must have been 50 of them. I recognised them as chinstrap penguins – there was a colony near Casey Station where we were staying. Like a platoon of little soldiers, the chinstraps marched resolutely towards the sea leopard.

'Wicked!' whispered Harry. 'They're going to kill the mean seal.'

'I doubt it,' I said. The sea leopard was much too big and powerful. When it saw the penguins coming, it snorted and bared its huge, leopard-like teeth.

But the silly little birds didn't falter. They continued waddling towards it. Towards their doom. Even more strange, many of the penguins – especially those at the rear – kept glancing back over their shoulders. As if the danger lay in that direction, not in front.

Suddenly there was a loud hiss behind us and a shower of big raindrops splattered on the ice. The whistling wind blew one across my cheek and into my mouth. It tasted salty. *Salty rain?*

'Look!' Harry pointed.

Fifteen metres from the floe, a circle of water roughly the size of a backyard pool bulged upwards like a giant bubble, then burst open in a spray of foam as an enormous black-and-white shape pushed up and out of the sea.

A killer whale.

For three or four seconds the huge head remained motionless, its rounded nose pointed straight up at the sky. Only its eye moved as the whale swept its gaze back and forth over the ice floe, then it sank back under the waves.

For a moment nothing moved. Every pair of eyes on the ice floe was focused on the spot where the killer whale had been.

Now I understood why the sea leopard wasn't interested in us. And why the penguins had jumped up onto the ice floe even though their deadly enemy was already there. Both the sea leopard and the penguins were trying to escape the killer whale.

At least they're safe now, I thought.

But I was wrong.

THUMP!

My feet shot out from under me as the far side of the ice floe rose three metres into the air. Holy guacamole! A huge, blurry shape pressed against the underside of the ice, lifting it up.

The killer whale was trying to tip us into the sea!

And it was succeeding. Everything on the ice – Harry, me, the sea leopard, the penguins – began sliding down the slope towards the dark, spiky waves.

'What's happening?' Harry gasped.

Before I could answer, another killer whale burst out of the sea on the low side of the floe. There were two of them. They were working as a team. The second giant predator flung itself onto the ice and came sliding up the slope on its belly with its mouth wide open. Straight towards Harry and me.

I had never seen so many teeth.

Harry and I started madly back-pedalling to stop ourselves from sliding into the whale's gaping jaws, but the weight of the huge animal tipped the floe even further and our boots couldn't grip.

'Shishkebab!' I cried, as we slid helplessly towards the enormous, tooth-lined cave of the killer whale's mouth.

5
NO ESCAPE

But the penguins slid faster. About ten of the little flightless birds went skidding past Harry and me, their stumpy wings flapping in panic, their orange feet clawing uselessly at the ice. The first eight or nine shot past the killer whale on both sides and made it safely into the sea before the huge predator had time to react. But it saw the next one coming. Rolling onto its side so the tip of its shiny black nose pushed flat against the ice, the whale opened its giant maw, then slammed it shut like a bank vault closing.

CLUNK!

I didn't see if it got the penguin. Harry and I were

locked together in a bear hug, doing a tandem roll across the tilt of the ice at right angles to the whale's line of attack. I knew we couldn't stop our slide; our only chance was to roll sideways.

It worked. Instead of going into the whale's mouth, we bumped into its head, just above the blowhole, and stopped sliding. For a moment I was looking directly into the whale's eye. It was as big as a light bulb.

I was staring straight at death.

Then the eye began to grow smaller. The whale had begun sliding backwards down the slope, wriggling itself from side to side to get off the ice. Finally, it turned almost all the way around and rolled into the waves with a five-metre-high splash.

As soon as the whale was gone, the floe tipped level again.

'You're squashing me!' squeaked a muffled voice.

I rolled off Harry and dragged him to his feet, nervously scanning the sea in all directions for killer whales. A tall black fin went cruising past.

'Quick, Harry,' I whispered. 'We have to get to the middle of the ice.'

'But the mean seal's there.'

Somehow the sea leopard had maintained its position in the centre of the ice floe. About 20 penguins – all that remained of the original 50 – crowded around it, huddled down on the ice like earthquake survivors expecting an aftershock.

'I don't think it'll hurt us,' I said. 'It's just as scared as we are.'

Hoping I was right, I cautiously led Harry towards it.

But we didn't get there.

THUMP!

It was a repeat performance. Harry and I landed flat on our backsides as the far side of the ice floe rose high into the air. All 20 remaining penguins – *and* the sea leopard – came sliding down the slope towards us. But they weren't getting any closer because Harry and I were sliding, too. I cast a panicked look over my shoulder. The sea came closer, closer, closer . . .

Something else was coming closer, too. Just below the water's surface, a huge black-and-white shape came powering towards the low side of the ice floe like a nuclear submarine at full throttle.

6
LOOK OUT!

This time there was no escape.

BANG! CRUNCH!

I have never been in a car crash, but now I know what it must be like: being T-boned by a rampaging killer whale when you're on an ice floe.

Everything happens so fast your brain can't keep up. But here's what I *think* happened. Seconds before the second whale hit, the ice floe broke in half. The first whale had lifted one side so high out of the water that the ice snapped across the middle like a sheet of glass.

That's what made the loud *BANG*.

The *CRUNCH* was the second whale smashing into the ice.

Moments earlier there had been a sloping ramp for it to toboggan up, but when the floe broke in half, the ice settled flat on the water again. Instead of sliding smoothly up a tilting plane of ice, the charging whale slammed headfirst into its hard, vertical edge like a seven-tonne battering ram. And smashed the floe into about ten pieces.

I found myself on one of the pieces. Lying flat on my back. Looking up at the sky.

Where was Harry?

I sat up quickly. *Too* quickly. The sudden movement caused the ice to tip alarmingly, nearly rolling me into the sea. A wave sloshed up onto the ice next to my hip. I shied away from it and nearly fell into the sea on the other side. Holy guacamole! I was sitting on a finger of ice barely wider than a kayak.

'Sam?'

My heart jumped. Harry was right behind me. Only three metres away. Crouched on the edge of another piece of ice that was much larger than the one I was on.

But he was sharing it with the sea leopard.

'Will I jump?' asked Harry, rising shakily to his feet.

'No! Stay where you are!' I said quickly. My floe was much too small to support us both. It barely supported me. Anyway, the gap was too wide to jump. Even for Captain Amazing.

'Sit down, Harry. I'll come to you.'

I pulled off my gloves and shoved them into my pockets. Then I lay on my belly and began paddling towards him.

Hooley dooley! The water was so cold it *burned*! It was like dipping my hands into liquid fire.

Ten times would have done it. I only had to dip my hands into the freezing water ten times and I would have paddled across to Harry. But I only got halfway before the sea erupted right in front of me.

WHOOSH!

A killer whale's head rose out of the water, so close I could smell its warm, fishy breath. I was a sitting duck. All it had to do was open its mouth a bit wider and I'd go straight in. But instead of eating me, the whale shot a column of vapour out of its blowhole and sank back into the sea.

'Holy torpedo, it nearly got you!' gasped Harry.

He was further away now. The turbulence caused by the breaching whale had turned my piece of ice side-on to Harry's and pushed us four metres apart. Four metres might not sound far, but when you're on a narrow sliver of ice and there's a pack of killer whales after you, it feels like four *kilometres*.

Trying not to splash too much, I slowly turned my ice kayak around. My skin prickled, and not from the cold. It *was* cold, of course, but not quite as cold as it had been five minutes earlier. The katabatic wind had died down completely, leaving the sea eerily flat and calm. A pale mist had fallen across the water. Except for my splashing hands and my wildly thumping heart, the scene was almost peaceful. Then Harry broke the quiet.

'LOOK OUT!'

7
WHAP! CRUNCH! SMACK!

I looked over my shoulder. Thirty metres away, a tall black fin came knifing through the water, dragging a V-shaped wave behind it.

I started paddling flat out. But I knew it was hopeless. How could I outrun a killer whale?

I was toast.

But I wasn't dead yet. As the saying goes – while there's life, there's hope.

And there's another saying, one that my karate teacher told me – attack is the best means of defence.

I stopped paddling and fumbled in my pocket, looking over my shoulder again to see how close the whale was.

It was *very* close. But, amazingly, it wasn't coming straight for me. If it held its present course, it would miss my narrow ice floe by a couple of metres. Then the realisation hit.

It was going for Harry!

'Oh no you don't!' I muttered through clenched teeth.

I waited until the huge predator was almost level with me, then hurled my glove.

One medium-sized, wool-lined Gore-Tex glove versus one seven-tonne killer whale. It doesn't take a genius to come up with a *no contest* result.

But tell the genius that the glove had just been dipped in seawater, so instead of weighing 200 grams, it now weighed two kilos. And that it had been aimed at the whale's most vulnerable spot – its eye.

WHAP!

I don't think I hurt it, but I did give the whale a fright. It flinched. And when it flinched, it veered off course – only by a few degrees, but enough to spoil its aim.

Instead of hitting Harry's ice floe dead-centre and spilling him and the sea leopard into the water, the whale struck the floe a glancing blow on one side. The ice floe rocked sideways and spun in a circle, nearly throwing Harry off. He slid all the way to the edge, only saving himself by grabbing one of the sea leopard's rear flippers. The big grey seal whirled around with its mouth wide open, but before it could close its terrible jaws around Harry's arm, another mouth – ten times bigger than the sea leopard's – exploded out of the sea.

The sea leopard might have looked slow and clumsy out of the water, but its reflexes were fast. Rearing up like a striking cobra, it bit the attacking whale on the point of its nose.

CRUNCH!

I didn't see what happened next. The whale's huge black-and-white tail rose out of the sea in front of me, blocking my view. Then it slammed down on the surface with a loud *SMACK*, sending up a curtain of water that nearly blew me off my ice kayak. By the time the spray had cleared, both the whale and the sea leopard had gone. Only Harry remained, lying white-faced on the edge of his ice floe.

'How cool was *that*!' he cried.

8
PIRATES

I paddled over to Harry's ice floe. The water was bone-crackingly cold. Every time I dipped my hands in, it felt like my fingers were about to drop off. But I was more worried about them being *bitten* off. And not just my fingers, my hands, arms and probably the rest of me as well. I'd seen up close how big a killer whale's mouth was.

Luckily the whales stayed away. But by the time I reached Harry, my hands were so numb with cold I couldn't use them. I got Harry to lie on his stomach and hold my ice kayak steady while I half-rolled, half-slid across onto the larger floe.

'Help me put my gloves back on,' I gasped. My hands

hurt so much I'd forgotten there was only one glove left. I couldn't even pull it out of my pocket. Harry had to do it for me, then thread the glove, one finger at a time, onto my freezing left hand. I felt as helpless as a baby. I clamped my bare right hand in my left armpit to warm it up. I was worried about frostbite. But more worried about the killer whales. Where were they?

Harry and I sat huddled in the middle of the ice floe, as far from the edge as possible. But it wasn't far enough and we both knew it. If the whales came back for us, we'd be an easy meal. There was no sea leopard to distract them now. No penguins. Just Harry and me, totally defenceless on our little raft of ice.

My eyes darted back and forth. At any moment I expected to see the tip of a fin, a V-shaped bow wave, a huge black-and-white head. But wherever the whales were, they weren't showing themselves. Nothing moved. The sea was dead calm. Everything was shrouded in mist, and visibility was down to a few hundred metres. I could no longer see land, only the dim shadows of icebergs.

Where were Dad and Ross? I wondered how far from shore we'd drifted. Now that the wind had died down, they might hear us if we shouted. I filled my lungs with icy air and cupped my hands around my mouth.

But before I could shout, I saw something that drove all thoughts of Dad and Ross from my mind – another shadow. One that wasn't an iceberg. One that was a lot darker than the soupy grey mist around it. A shadow that grew steadily larger.

Harry had noticed it, too. 'Uh oh!' he said. 'Killer whale.'

I shook my head. My heart started beating really fast. Not from fear this time, but excitement.

'Listen,' I said.

Carrying faintly across the water came the most beautiful sound I'd ever heard – the throb of a diesel engine.

Harry and I scrambled to our feet and started yelling and waving. Out of the mist came a small, squat ship, painted completely black and streaked with rust.

Harry and I stopped yelling and slowly lowered our arms.

Hanging limp from a pole at the front of the approaching vessel was a skull-and-crossbones flag.

'Holy torpedo!' breathed Harry. 'Pirates!'

9
CAPTAIN DAN

I could hardly believe my eyes. OK, I knew pirates still existed, but the last place I expected them to be was Antarctica. Who would they steal stuff from?

Just then a figure appeared on the foredeck – a stout, bearded man wearing a red exposure suit with its hood pulled up. He looked more like Santa Claus than a pirate.

'Ahoy there!' he called in an accent that was unmistakably American. 'Are you from the plane crash?'

I realised the pirates must have intercepted Ross's Mayday call and come to plunder the wreckage.

'Yes,' I yelled back. 'Will you help us?'

'Pleased to oblige, buddy.'

The pirate ship came to a stop about 40 metres away. Painted on the bow in dribbly red letters was the ship's name – *Black Pimpernel*. Four yellow-clad figures lowered a Zodiac inflatable boat into the water. Santa Claus and a much smaller figure clambered down a rope ladder into it and came motoring towards us. As they drew closer, I saw that the small pirate was a girl. She manoeuvred the bobbing craft skilfully alongside our ice floe.

'What happened to the others?' the big pirate asked as he tossed me a rope.

I caught it in my gloved left hand. 'They made it ashore,' I said, studying him closely. He looked vaguely familiar. 'But there's nothing left of the plane.' *Nothing worth plundering*, I nearly added.

'Are you a pirate?' asked Harry.

Our unlikely rescuer let out a loud, Santa-like laugh. 'There are people who call me that,' he said with a chuckle. 'But I only worry about what the whales say.'

Harry screwed up his face. 'Whales don't *talk*!'

'You're dead right there, buddy. That's why me and my pirate gang' – he winked at the girl pirate – 'have to act on their behalf.'

44

I frowned at Santa Claus. The rope that connected us was literally a lifeline. If he let go, Harry and I would drift away into the Southern Ocean, never to be seen again. Then I remembered where I recognised him from – *Earth Watch* magazine.

'Are you that guy who saves whales?'

He gave a little bow. 'Captain Dan Caldwell at your service, gentlemen. And who might you be?'

As Captain Dan and the girl helped us into the Zodiac and gave us life jackets to put on, I told them who we were and how our ski plane had been forced to make an emergency landing on the ice.

'We were the nearest vessel when your Mayday call went out,' Captain Dan said. 'But the *Black Pimpernel* was never built for speed. We nearly burst a boiler trying to get here in time.'

The girl gave me her woollen scarf to wrap around my half-frozen right hand. She was quite short and looked barely older than me. I thought she might be Captain Dan's granddaughter. But when she spoke, her accent wasn't American, it was European. 'For sure, you boys must be freezing cold,' she said. 'We will go back to the ship and find you some dry clothes and a nice hot drink.'

'We're dry enough,' I said politely, turning to Captain Dan. 'Can we rescue Dad and Mr Willis now?'

Captain Dan frowned into the thickening mist. It hung all around us like a damp grey curtain. 'We can't be more than half a mile from shore,' he said in his slow American drawl. He turned to the girl. 'What do you think, Frøya? Can you find your way through this pea souper?'

Frøya settled herself next to the outboard motor. 'For sure, I can try.'

As Frøya steered the Zodiac carefully through a crazy paving of bobbing ice floes, Captain Dan had a call on his two-way radio from someone called Billy aboard the *Black Pimpernel*. I couldn't hear what Billy was saying, but it made Captain Dan very excited.

'OK, we're on our way.' He lowered the radio. 'Take us back to the ship, Frøya, and don't spare the horses. We've got us some Japanese whalers to put out of business.'

'Wicked!' said Harry.

'What about Dad and Mr Willis?' I asked as Frøya turned the Zodiac around and headed back the way we'd come.

'They'll be OK,' Captain Dan replied. 'Billy McCormack,

my first officer, says there's a rescue helicopter on its way from Casey Station.'

'Will they be able to find them in this fog?'

Captain Dan nodded. 'With all the tracking equipment they have on those rescue choppers, they could find a needle in a haystack.'

It wasn't a needle I was worried about; it was my dad. But I knew I'd be wasting my breath arguing with Captain Dan when there was a choice between going back for my father or saving some whales from Japanese harpoon boats. According to the article I'd read about him in *Earth Watch*, he cared more about whales than anything else in the world. Already he was back on the two-way radio, talking to his first officer about coordinates and engine speed and how much fuel was left in the *Black Pimpernel*'s tanks.

'What about Harry and me?' I asked as the rusty, black anti-whaling ship loomed ahead of us in the mist.

Captain Dan gave us a puzzled look, as if he'd forgotten who we were and what we were doing aboard one of his Zodiacs.

'Ever been on a pirate ship?' he asked.

10
MURDERERS

The *Black Pimpernel* even had cannons – *water* cannons. There were two on the foredeck, six along each side and another two in the stern. Captain Dan and his crew used them to defend the ship from unwanted boarders. They had other weapons, too – catapults to hurl bottles of butter acid and smokebombs onto the decks of whaling ships; prop foulers to tangle their propellers; and the 'can opener', a two-metre-long steel blade attached to the bow to slice open their hulls. The *Black Pimpernel* really was a pirate ship!

'But it's the whalers who are doing the crime,' Frøya said as she set two mugs of hot chocolate and a plate of scones in front of Harry and me in the ship's galley. 'Sure, they say it is research, but they do not kill 1,000 protected whales every year for science! It is for whale meat that they are doing this horrible murder – whale meat for the fancy restaurants all over Japan.'

'What does whale meat taste like?' asked Harry, helping himself to one of the doughy cheese scones.

Frøya flicked the long blonde hair out of her eyes. 'I would die rather than eat it,' she said fiercely. 'Whales are beautiful creatures, so calm and gentle.'

I thought about the pod of killer whales that nearly ate Harry and me for breakfast, but decided not to mention it. 'Is it dangerous sailing with Captain Dan?'

'Do not worry, Sam. A helicopter will come and get you boys before we reach the whaling ship.'

I was disappointed. I'd been looking forward to using a water cannon. 'Do you know if they found Dad and Mr Willis?'

'I will go and hear if there is news.' Frøya disappeared up a narrow flight of stairs, leaving Harry and me in the galley with Spiro, the ship's cook, who was stirring a big urn of seafood soup on the stove.

'Is Frøya a pirate, too?' Harry whispered. He wore a blue-and-white jumper that belonged to Frøya, and a pair of yellow ski-trousers about four sizes too big for him.

I laughed. 'No, she isn't a pirate.' Frøya had found me a change of clothes, too, which fitted me better than Harry's. 'And neither is Captain Dan,' I added. 'They're environmentalists – they stop people from killing whales.'

Harry sipped his hot chocolate. 'Killing whales is bad, isn't it, Sam?'

'That's right,' I said, taking a bite of scone.

'Even killer whales?'

The half-frozen fingers of my right hand began to sting and tingle as the blood seeped back into them. I wrapped them around my mug for extra warmth.

'Even killer whales,' I said.

'Good news, boys.' Frøya came clattering down the companionway two stairs at a time. 'Billy called the helicopter on the radio. They have rescued your father and the pilot. They are both OK.'

That was a relief. I'd been worried about Dad getting hypothermia after falling through the ice.

'Will the helicopter come and get us now?' asked Harry.

'There is bad news, also,' Frøya said with a sigh. 'A big storm is coming, so the helicopter must go quickly to Casey Station before the weather becomes too bad for flying.'

'Will Captain Dan take us back there?'

Frøya shrugged. 'For three weeks we have searched for the Japanese whaling ships and at last we have found them. I am thinking Captain Dan will not turn back just yet.'

There was a rumble under our feet. The *Black Pimpernel* shook like a huge waking animal as its diesel engine chugged into life.

'So Harry and me are stuck on board?' I said.

Frøya nodded apologetically.

'Wicked!' Harry and I both said at the same time.

11
SCREAMING
SIXTIES

I'd been excited when Frøya told us we were stuck on the *Black Pimpernel* on account of the approaching storm. But I didn't think it through. I was thinking about water cannons and smokebombs and going to war against Japanese whaling ships; I *wasn't* thinking about the storm itself. We were at sea in the Antarctic Circle, in a region known as the Screaming Sixties – the coldest, windiest, most inhospitable place on Earth – and the *Black Pimpernel* was only a small ship.

Not the best situation to be in.

Especially if you get seasick.

I didn't know I got seasick until ten minutes after

the storm hit. Suddenly I lost all my hot chocolate – and two cheese scones – into a red plastic bucket that Spiro gave me when he saw the colour of my face. ('You is turn green,' he told me.) Thirty seconds later, I lost my breakfast as well. Then I lost what remained of the previous night's dinner. Pretty soon, nothing was left in my stomach but an achey hollow feeling. And still I kept throwing up.

Seasickness is about the worst you can feel and still be alive.

Nobody else on the ship was seasick. Not even Harry.

'Gross!' he said, the first time I spewed. As if I could help it.

After my second time, Harry said, 'I'm out of here,' and went up to the bridge to see what Captain Dan was doing.

I stayed below deck. For the first hour or two I spent most of my time in the *Black Pimpernel*'s smallest room (it's called the 'head' on a ship), clinging to the toilet bowl to stop myself being flung against the walls by the trampolining motion of the giant waves. When I'd stopped being sick, I crawled with my bucket to a spare cabin, lay down on the narrow bunk and waited to die.

I *felt* like I was going to die – either from seasickness or when the ship sank. It seemed impossible that the *Black Pimpernel* could survive the terrible pounding of the wild seas. When Frøya described the approaching storm as big, she hadn't been kidding. It was HUGE. A force ten gale. With winds strong enough to flatten a house. Or toss a ship around like a rubber duck in a washing machine. I clung to my bunk to stop myself being thrown off, while around me the *Black Pimpernel* heaved and shuddered and groaned. It sounded like it was about to break into bits.

But the old girl hung together. She didn't capsize and she didn't sink. And I didn't die.

A hand touched my shoulder. 'Sam, how are you feeling?' Frøya asked.

'Sick as a dog.'

'Come upstairs and you will feel better.'

'I'm not going outside in this weather,' I groaned.

'For sure, we will not go outside,' she laughed. 'Come with me up to the bridge.'

I didn't want to go anywhere. But before I could object, Frøya hauled me to my feet. She was surprisingly strong for someone so small. With one arm around my waist and the other holding my bucket, she led me swerving and swaying down a long narrow gangway. We bumped from wall to wall like marbles in a pinball machine. Halfway along, we passed a porthole. I shouldn't have looked out. Hooley dooley! The horizon is supposed to be level. This one wasn't. It was tipped 45 degrees from the horizontal. Then, as I watched, it slowly swung a full 90 degrees in the other direction.

'Give me the bucket!' I gasped.

A minute later Frøya guided me through a low doorway into the dining room, which she called the 'mess'. It was crowded. About 20 men and women, most of them not much older than Frøya, sat around the long, bolted-down tables, calmly eating their lunch. They had to hold their bowls clear of the tables to stop the contents from slopping out. The mess *reeked* of seafood soup. I couldn't get out of there fast enough.

There were three people on the bridge – Captain Dan, a tall skinny man standing at the helm who turned out to be First Officer Billy McCormack, and Harry. There was also the same gut-turning stink of seafood. At first

I thought the horrible smell must have followed Frøya and me up from the mess, then I noticed two empty bowls on a tray in one corner. A third bowl rested in Harry's lap. He looked quite at home eating his soup in the captain's chair, eyes glued to a glowing green radar screen set into a console above his head.

How come he *doesn't get seasick?* I wondered.

'Come check out the Japanese ships,' Harry said when he noticed me.

I lurched across the swaying floor towards him. The bridge was two storeys above the main deck, so the pitch and roll of the giant seas felt worse than downstairs. I had to grab the back of the captain's chair to stop myself falling over. Like everything else on the *Black Pimpernel*, it was firmly bolted down.

'See those two big dots?' Harry said, pointing with his spoon. 'They're Japanese whaling ships.'

Trying my best to ignore the fishy smell floating up from his soup bowl, I looked at the two green blips on the radar. For the first time since the storm hit, I forgot about my seasickness.

'How far away are they?'

Captain Dan made his way over from the chart table and stood at my shoulder, supporting himself against a bulkhead. 'About 15 kilometres. They're only doing four and a half knots, riding out the storm. If they don't see us coming, we should catch up with them in a couple of hours.'

'Then what will we do?' I asked, thinking about water cannons again.

'There's nothing we can do until the storm passes,' Captain Dan said. He had to raise his voice above the howl of the 180 km/h wind that pummelled the bridge's reinforced windows and shrieked through the superstructure outside. 'It would be too dangerous to get close in this weather. But in the meantime, the storm is working in our favour. Billy is running us with the waves. I'm hoping the Japanese will mistake us for an iceberg on their radar.'

I thought of the *Titanic*. How it hit an iceberg and sank. 'Are there many icebergs out here?'

'Thousands,' said Captain Dan, indicating a rash of tiny blips across the screen that I'd mistaken for waves. 'But with Billy at the helm, we're safe as houses.'

I hoped he was right. I certainly didn't *feel* safe. The *Black Pimpernel*'s bow reared skywards as it climbed another watery mountain, then plunged sickeningly down the other side. When we hit the bottom, the splash was so big that the forward half of the ship disappeared in a massive explosion of spray and foam.

'Whoopeeeeee!' yelled Harry, holding his half-full bowl of soup out in front of him and somehow not spilling a drop.

The other three people on the bridge – Frøya, Captain Dan and Billy – laughed.

I made a wild grab for my bucket.

12
COLLISION
COURSE

Two and a half hours later we had our first glimpse of the Japanese ships. Or one of them, anyway. The storm had passed, but a veil of misty rain and gently falling snow made it hard to see. Captain Dan peered through his binoculars at a huge grey shape looming directly ahead.

'I think it's the factory ship, the *Nisshin Maru*,' he said. 'We're coming up astern of her. They don't know we're here.'

'Where's the killer ship, Captain?' asked Billy.

Captain Dan studied the radar screen. 'About a mile to the north. We'll deal with the *Nisshin* first, then go looking for her.'

'Sink them, Captain Dan!' cried Harry.

'Shhh,' I said softly. This was a tense moment. Captain Dan had a ship to command and he might send Harry and me below deck if we got in the way.

Frøya came over and stood next to us. 'Captain Dan does not actually *sink* whaling ships, Harry,' she whispered. 'He just stops them from murdering whales.'

'How?'

'You will see,' said Frøya.

Slowly, the huge Japanese factory ship materialised out of the murk. It was still several hundred metres away. I could see an orange helicopter on the afterdeck and, below it, the wide, blood-stained ramp cut into her stern where they winched the dead whales out of the sea. The sight of it turned my stomach, but I was over my seasickness now that the storm had passed.

'Shall we ram them with the can opener, Captain?' asked Billy, making a minor adjustment to the *Black Pimpernel*'s helm.

Captain Dan lowered his binoculars. 'Only as a last resort, Billy. I think we'll try the prop foulers first, then hit them with the butter acid and smokebombs.'

He turned to Frøya. 'Tell the prop-fouler crew to man their stations. But everybody's to keep their heads down till I give the order. I want to take them by surprise.'

'For sure,' said Frøya, and raced downstairs.

'Billy, see if you can get around in front of her.'

'Aye aye, Captain.'

Down on the bow, the Jolly Roger flapped in the breeze as Billy spun the helm to the right. It was really exciting. Like being in a movie. We rocked over the *Nisshin Maru*'s wake and headed straight for the whale ramp. There was a pinkish-brown stain in the water and the sickening smell of death in the air. My excitement turned to anger when I thought of the hundreds of dead whales that had been dragged up that ramp and butchered for the Japanese fish markets.

Billy spun the helm again, taking us around the factory ship's stern and along its starboard side. It dwarfed us. All I could see was a wall of steel. Painted along the *Nisshin Maru*'s side in huge white letters, each one as tall as our radio mast, was a single word in English:

RESEARCH

Frøya's words came back to me: *Sure, they say it is*

research, but they do not kill 1,000 protected whales every year for science!

Harry and I had come to Antarctica because we'd won first prize in a raffle to raise funds for wildlife conservation, not to actually *do* anything for wildlife conservation. But fate had landed us aboard the *Black Pimpernel*, and now I had a chance to get involved.

'Should I go down to the water cannons, Captain Dan?'

He looked at me and frowned, and I knew immediately that I should have taken my own advice to Harry and not attracted attention to myself.

'How old are you, bud?'

'Fourteen.'

'A babe in the woods!'

'I'll be turning 15 in a couple of months,' I said, desperate to convince him. 'And I know my way around boats. My uncle has a houseboat and we spend two weeks every summer cruising up and down the Murray River.'

Captain Dan flipped a switch on the console above his head. He wasn't even listening. 'Tell you what, bud. Why don't you and your brother – '

I knew what he was going to say: *Why don't you and*

your brother go below deck where you'll be out of the way and not in any danger of falling overboard.

But he never got to say it. Because suddenly there was the blast of a ship's horn – *Hoot! Hoot! Hoot!* – and the sound of a whistle blowing. Behind us, white water boiled around the *Nisshin Maru*'s stern as the huge, underwater props powered up to maximum revs.

'We've been spotted,' said the first officer.

Captain Dan strode to the window on the port wing of the bridge. 'Put the hammer down, Billy. Give it everything we've got.'

Billy pushed the throttle lever to full power. There was a rumble under our feet and the *Black Pimpernel* surged forward.

It was a race. The *Nisshin Maru* had a higher top speed than Captain Dan's old rust bucket, but we'd caught the whalers napping. They had been idling along at only four and a half knots when they spotted us; we were doing twice that. Gradually we overtook them and pulled ahead of the *Nisshin Maru*'s huge curved bow. Billy kept us on a steady course until 300 metres of clear water separated the two vessels. Then Captain Dan gave an order that chilled my blood.

'Thirty degrees to port, Billy.'

To port, I thought. Wasn't that left? But the *Nisshin Maru* was on our left!

Sure enough, the first officer spun the wheel to the left. And the *Black Pimpernel* turned slowly across the path of the approaching giant.

Now the Japanese ship was coming straight towards us. Even though it was 300 metres away, it looked as big as a mountain. Its captain blasted the horn, warning us to get out of the way.

'They're going to smash into us!' Harry whispered, his eyes big with fright.

I put my arm around him. It *did* look like the two vessels were going to collide. But both Billy and Captain Dan seemed perfectly calm. Captain Dan reached for a microphone.

'Deploy the prop foulers!' he commanded, his voice booming from a pair of loudspeakers mounted above the bridge.

Below us, a team of crewmen wearing bright-yellow dry suits swarmed out on deck and rushed back towards the stern. They began heaving coils of thick black rope with floats attached into the churning grey sea behind the *Black Pimpernel*'s stern.

'What are they doing?' Harry asked.

'They're trying to tangle the *Nisshin*'s propellers,' I said. Frøya had explained it to me earlier. 'If it works, the factory ship will have to be towed back to Japan for repairs and they won't be able to kill any more whales.'

But I wondered if Captain Dan had left it too late. The *Nisshin Maru* was 150 metres away, rushing towards us at full speed.

Hoot! Hoot! Hoot! went its horn.

'Collision, 45 seconds!' Captain Dan's voice boomed over the loudspeakers.

It confirmed my worst fears. The *Nisshin Maru* was going to T-bone us.

We'd be cut in half!

13
BOMB CREW, DO YOUR STUFF!

The *Nisshin Maru*'s huge reinforced bow came slicing through the sea like a giant axe. It was going to hit us mid ship. We'd go straight to the bottom.

'Should I turn?' Billy asked.

'Hold your course,' said Captain Dan, as cool as a cucumber. It was a deadly game of 'chicken' on the high seas. He pulled the microphone close to his mouth.

'Collision, 30 seconds!'

More crewmen in life jackets rushed out on deck below us.

Hoot! Hoot! Hoot! went the *Nisshin Maru*'s horn.

Even though the temperature on the poorly heated

bridge was only a few degrees above freezing, I was sweating. Harry slipped his hand into mine.

'Collision, 20 seconds!' Captain Dan's steely voice boomed across the ship.

Then the Japanese captain lost his nerve. With its horn blaring angrily, the oncoming juggernaut began to turn left. But a ship weighing 8,000 tonnes can't change direction quickly. It wasn't going to turn in time!

'Should I let her through?' asked Billy, beads of sweat glistening on his forehead as the *Nisshin Maru* loomed huge on our port side.

'Hold your course,' said Captain Dan. 'They're trying to turn inside us to avoid the prop foulers.'

Hoot! Hoot! Hoot! Hoot! went the *Nisshin Maru*. It grew bigger, bigger, BIGGER, until I could see nothing else out the window.

I held my breath as the factory ship's massive curved bow swung right overhead. It blocked out the sky. All of us on the bridge, except Captain Dan, instinctively ducked our heads, waiting for the smashing impact that would send us to the bottom.

It didn't come. Miraculously, the *Nisshin Maru* swept past barely ten metres from the *Black Pimpernel*'s port side.

'Looks like the prop foulers didn't work,' Captain Dan said as the Japanese ship slowly overtook us.

The two ships were side by side.

Captain Dan reached for the microphone. 'Butter acid and smokebomb crews, do your stuff!'

I watched enviously as a dozen yellow-clad figures raced up onto the foredeck. Using hand-held catapults, they started firing bottles and smoking canisters up towards the *Nisshin Maru*'s deck.

'Wicked!' said Harry. 'Blow them up!'

Captain Dan laughed. 'Nobody will be blown up, young Harry. But there'll be a few sore eyes and runny noses on board their ship tonight.'

Not as many as there should be, I thought. Half the missiles didn't make it over the *Nisshin Maru*'s rail. Instead, they bounced off the hull and fell harmlessly into the sea, trailing plumes of orange smoke behind them. I might have been only 14 – a *babe in the woods* – but I knew I could do a better job than many of the bomb crew.

'Can I have a go, Captain?'

'No, bud, this isn't a game,' the captain said. He clicked the microphone back on. 'Tagging detail to the main deck. I think her paintwork needs a touch up.'

Four crew members dragged a compressor and a ten-litre tin of paint to the rail and began spraying bright-orange lines onto the *Nisshin Maru*'s side. It wasn't until the lines joined and became a huge dribbly **M** that I realised the tagging detail was writing a word. Next came a two-metre-high **U**, then an **R**. But they didn't get the next letter finished – it was going to be a **D** – before the factory ship began drawing away from the smaller, less powerful *Black Pimpernel*, leaving us rocking in its wake like a child's bath toy.

MUR it said on the *Nisshin Maru*'s hull, half obliterating the bogus **RESEARCH** sign that was already there.

'Nice work, taggers,' Captain Dan said over the loudspeakers. 'With any luck, you'll get to finish your artwork a bit later on.'

As the factory ship sailed away, I saw a tall black fin break the surface just behind its blood-stained spillway.

The sight of it made my skin prickle.

'Look – a killer whale!'

'They often hang around whaling ships,' Billy said. 'They feed on the shoals of fish attracted by the blood from the butchered whales.'

'Eeew!' said Harry.

Captain Dan's voice boomed over the loudspeakers again: 'C Crew and D Crew, prepare Zodiacs for launch.'

There was a frenzy of activity on the deck below us. Within a couple of minutes, two Zodiacs, each with a crew of four, went charging off after the *Nisshin Maru*. The Zodiacs were faster than the *Black Pimpernel*; they could keep up with the factory ship.

'What will they do?' asked Harry.

'Lay another prop fouler across their bow, if they can,' Captain Dan said. 'And chuck a few more smokebombs. Basically, just give the whale butchers a hard time so they get the message that they're not wanted here.'

As the Japanese factory ship and the two tiny pursuit craft disappeared into the mist, Captain Dan switched the radio to an open maritime channel. '*Nisshin Maru*, *Nisshin Maru*, this is *Black Pimpernel*. You are in violation of international whaling laws. Killing whales for human consumption is a criminal act. Next time we meet, I'll put you out of business for good!'

'I wish you'd sunk them,' Harry muttered.

'They nearly sank *us*!' said Billy, wiping his brow. 'That was a really close call.'

Captain Dan winked at Harry and me. 'I haven't lost a game of chicken yet.'

'What if you *had* lost?' I asked.

'The Japanese captain and his officers would have gone to prison. We were on their starboard, so we had right of way.'

'Were you worried they weren't going to give way?'

'A bit,' Captain Dan admitted. 'But it would've created such an international incident that it might have ended Japanese whaling forever. So either way, I couldn't lose.'

'You could have lost your life.'

'We all could have lost our lives,' Captain Dan said grimly. 'And I apologise for putting you and your brother at risk. But in the long run, losing our lives might have saved the lives of thousands of whales. A fair exchange, don't you think?'

14
FREAK OUT

Would it be a fair exchange? I wondered. Sacrificing the lives of everyone on board the *Black Pimpernel* for the lives of thousands of whales? I didn't know if I would risk my life to save even one whale.

Anyway, Captain Dan wasn't going to give me the chance. Ever since he had found out my age, he'd treated me like a little kid. It was frustrating. I wouldn't have missed the *Nisshin Maru*'s deck if I'd been one of the smokebomb crew.

Frøya came puffing back up the stairs to the bridge. Her bright-yellow dry suit was flecked with orange paint. She must have been one of the tagging detail.

'Four of the men are sick, Captain,' she said.

Captain Dan turned from the chart table. 'What are the symptoms?'

'Vomiting and diarrhoea.'

'Excuse me, Captain, could you take the helm?' Billy asked. His face had turned white. 'I don't feel so good.' He staggered across the bridge and disappeared below deck.

Captain Dan took over the wheel. He was a bit pale, too. 'Looks like food poisoning,' he muttered. 'It must be that seafood soup we had for lunch.'

'I didn't have any,' said Frøya. She'd told me earlier that she was vegetarian.

'Me neither,' I said.

But Harry did. There was a gurgling sound at my elbow and Harry charged across the bridge to my bucket. He got there just in time.

Captain Dan burped and rubbed his stomach. 'It looks like we're going to need a lot of buckets,' he said.

Thirty-nine, to be exact. And eight more when the two Zodiacs came back. They had to break off their pursuit of the *Nisshin Maru* because everyone got sick.

In the space of half an hour, the *Black Pimpernel* went from being an anti-whaling ship to a hospital ship.

Everyone on board except Frøya and me had food poisoning from the contaminated seafood soup.

Frøya wasn't very sympathetic. 'We are supposed to be on the same side as the sea creatures,' she said. 'Should we really be eating them?'

It was a difficult question. One that I didn't have much time to think about because I had other things on my mind. Like how to drive a ship.

The food poisoning was so nasty that even Captain Dan had to go below deck. He left Frøya and me on the bridge with orders to maintain our present course and speed until he came back. He said he'd only be gone five minutes. But five minutes ticked by, then ten, then 15, and still he wasn't back. After nearly half an hour, Frøya went looking for him, leaving me at the helm. Captain Sam. In charge of a 50-metre pirate ship.

Cool!

I would have enjoyed it more, except there were three icebergs ahead and the middle one was directly in our path. Should I go around it, or slow down?

Either way I'd be disobeying Captain Dan's orders, but I was alone on the bridge and the safety of the *Black*

Pimpernel and its crew was in my hands. There were 49 people on board, including my five-year-old brother, whom Frøya and I had carried below deck and put to bed in an empty cabin. It was a big responsibility.

The iceberg was big, too – roughly the size of the Sydney Opera House. If we ran into it, it would be *Titanic* all over again.

I made my decision and spun the wheel to starboard.

'Steady as you go,' I muttered as the *Black Pimpernel* began to veer slowly to the right. It was as easy as driving my uncle's houseboat.

When the gently flapping Jolly Roger on the bow was lined up with the gap between the middle iceberg and the one on the right, I straightened the wheel. The gap was easily wide enough to fit through.

Doing a steady eight knots, the *Black Pimpernel* motored towards the gap. I turned it a few degrees to port so we would pass dead centre between the two icebergs. The ship came around nicely. Being a sea captain wasn't so difficult.

From 100 metres away the icebergs looked magnificent. They rose out of the sea like cliffs of cut glass, glowing blue-green where the light shone through them. I wished Mum was there to see it. I wished she could see me at the controls of an actual ship. She'd freak out!

Then I saw something that nearly freaked *me* out.

Penguins. There were about 20 of them in the middle of the gap between the two icebergs. And here's the freaky part – *they were standing on the water*! I wasn't fooled. Even penguins can't do that.

So what were they standing on?

Shishkebab!

An underwater bridge of ice stretched across from one towering iceberg to the other. It was the same blueish colour as the sea, so I wouldn't have noticed it if not for the penguins.

The icebergs were joined. It wasn't two icebergs like I'd first thought, it was *one* iceberg. With a valley in the middle and a towering peak at each end. I knew enough about icebergs to know that most of the ice was beneath the surface, hanging in the water like an upside-down mountain range.

And the *Black Pimpernel* was going to plough straight into it!

15
GO DOWN FIGHTING

It was too late to turn. I grabbed the throttle lever and pulled it back as far as it would go. There was a rumble under my feet and the *Black Pimpernel* trembled from stem to stern as its propeller went into reverse. We started slowing down, but not fast enough. Penguins scooted right and left as the edge of the ice came rushing towards the ship and disappeared under its bow.

CRUNCH!

The impact threw me across the bridge. I slammed into the forward bulkhead and hit my head on the window. For a moment I saw stars. I gripped the window ledge to hold myself up.

It was noisy. The initial, bone-jarring *crunch* of impact had been replaced by a creaking noise that seemed to reverberate around the whole ship. I felt a shaking sensation through the soles of my boots. The floor didn't seem level. I blinked to clear my vision. My face was pressed against the window and my breath fogged the glass. I wiped it clear with my elbow.

The first thing I saw was the grinning skull of the Jolly Roger flag. It was much higher than it should have been – nearly level with the bridge.

The *Black Pimpernel* was a converted fishing trawler, not an icebreaker. When it hit the ice, its bow had ridden up onto the ice shelf. Now it was stuck there, with its bow high in the air and its stern under water.

So much for my career as a sea captain. Five minutes at the helm and I'd run us aground.

Except it wasn't ground we were stuck on, it was ice. And the ice was cracking.

CREEEEEEEEAK!

I looked up in the direction of the noise.

Uh oh!

Two enormous cliffs of ice loomed overhead – one

on either side of the stranded ship's bow. They were the two ice peaks I had mistaken for separate icebergs. Now the *Black Pimpernel* was right underneath them. And – *CREEEEEEAK!* – a long, zigzagging crack ran from the ship's bow, across the ice bridge and up the side of one of them. It was almost all the way to the top, and growing wider every moment.

I could see what was about to happen. As soon as the crack reached the top, a chunk of ice weighing several thousand tonnes was going to break away from the cliff face and fall. It would land directly on top of us.

The *Black Pimpernel* would be flattened.

CREEEEEEEEAK!

I was alone on the ship's bridge. Where was Captain Dan? Where was Frøya? Until they returned, I was in charge. The safety of the ship and the lives of everyone aboard was in my hands. And what was I doing?

Nothing.

But what *could* I do?

The ship was stuck on the ice like a beached whale. *Like a killer whale on an ice floe*, said a little voice in my head. That gave me an idea.

Remembering how the killer whale that attacked Harry and me had wriggled from side to side to get off the ice floe, I raced back to the *Black Pimpernel*'s wheel and spun it as far as I could to the right. Then I spun it left.

Nothing seemed to happen. The engine was in full reverse, but its single propeller couldn't get enough grip on the water to drag the 800-tonne ship off the ice. I spun the helm back to the right. My hands were sweaty on the polished knobs of the big wooden wheel and my arm muscles were tingling.

CREEEEEEEEEAK!

High overhead, the crack had nearly reached the top of the ice cliff.

Heart racing, I spun the wheel the other way.

A slight tremor ran through the ship and there was a grinding noise under my feet. Did the *Black Pimpernel* move, or had I just imagined it?

I spun the wheel again.

'Sam, what has happened?'

Frøya was halfway up the companionway, straining to support Captain Dan, who leaned heavily on her shoulder. He didn't look well. His face was as white as the ice outside and his eyes looked bloodshot and glazed.

'Give me . . . a hand . . . bud,' he groaned.

I shook my head. 'Sorry. Too busy,' and spun the wheel as far as it would turn to the right. I was disobeying a direct order from the ship's captain, but there was not a moment to lose. One eye on the wall of ice hanging over us, I began spinning the helm back to the left.

And the floor beneath my feet moved – just a fraction – to the right.

I spun the helm the other way and felt another slight movement through the soles of my boots.

There was a grinding noise and the *Black Pimpernel* slid backwards two or three centimetres. I spun the wheel again. We slid back five more centimetres. I was sweating inside my exposure suit; it takes a lot of effort to turn the helm of a ship and my arms felt like they were going to drop off, but I didn't stop turning the wheel. Left, right, left, right. Slowly the ship was wriggling off the ice, just like the killer whale had done, only slower.

Too slow.

CREEEEEEEEEAK!

Then there was an ominous silence.

The crack had reached the top of the cliff! A huge section of the iceberg broke away and started tilting outwards. It blocked out the sky.

Both Frøya and Captain Dan saw the shadow and turned their faces skywards.

Nobody said a word. We all knew we were going to die.

But I kept spinning the wheel. Left, right, left, right.

The *Black Pimpernel* ground backwards another ten centimetres.

Still leaning on Frøya, Captain Dan staggered up the last of the stairs. He lurched across the bridge and reached for the wheel, but I blocked him with my elbow.

'Sorry, Captain,' I said. If he was too weak to climb the stairs on his own, no way was he strong enough to spin the helm.

I had got us into this mess; it was up to me to get us out of it.

Or I would go down fighting.

16
SAVE US!

There wasn't a crash or a boom, just a deafening roar that went on and on as several thousand tonnes of ice and snow exploded across the *Black Pimpernel*'s bow. The floor dropped under my feet like a lift that's broken its cable, then heaved back up again. It would have thrown me across the bridge if I hadn't been gripping the helm. Frøya and Captain Dan crashed into the chart table and fell in a heap on the floor. A broken radio mast toppled past the window, but other than that nothing was visible outside. The world had turned completely blue.

My heart did a backflip. We were underwater!

Then the roaring stopped and I saw why everything

was blue. It wasn't water outside the window, it was ice. The *Black Pimpernel* was crawling backwards through the choppy sea with a chunk of iceberg the size of a house resting crookedly on her main deck. The weight of it was slowly tipping us sideways.

'We're going to capsize!' cried Frøya. She tried to stand up but her left ankle gave out under her and she sat heavily back down on the floor.

Captain Dan didn't say anything. Perhaps he was too stunned to speak. He just looked at me across the steeply sloping bridge, and I thought I saw a pleading look in his eyes. A look that said: *Save us!*

But I didn't know what to do. I'd reversed the *Black Pimpernel* off the ice, escaping the full force of the icefall, but part of the collapsing iceberg had somehow ended up on our deck and it was going to roll us over.

You save us, I wanted to say to Captain Dan, but he was obviously too weak and groggy to do anything. And Frøya had hurt her ankle. So everyone's fate was still in my hands.

But I no longer wanted the responsibility. Captain Dan was right – I was only a boy. I'd *tried* to save us and look what had happened!

It no longer felt cool to be Captain Sam.

A large wave rolled under the *Black Pimpernel*'s hull and we tipped even further to starboard. Another few degrees and we'd capsize for sure.

I had to do *something*.

But what?

The ship was still in reverse. I couldn't go forward because the ice chunk on the deck made it impossible to see what lay in front of us. But I could turn.

I looked out the rear window to check that all was clear, then spun the wheel as far to the right as it would go. The reversing ship went into a sharp starboard turn. Just as I'd hoped, the tilt lessened by two or three degrees and held there – the turn was counteracting the sideways lean caused by the ice chunk. As long as I kept reversing the ship in circles, we wouldn't tip over. But I knew we couldn't keep it up forever. Eventually we would either run out of petrol or run into an iceberg.

I grabbed the radio to call for help, but I couldn't make it work. The radio mast had been sheared off by the falling ice. We were on our own.

Think, Sam, think!

There were icebergs all around us. Several of them were small – chunks that had broken off the falling ice wall and landed in the sea – but there were some big ones, too. One of them was almost as large as the Sydney Opera House. It looked familiar, except now there was no longer an underwater bridge connecting it to the one next to it. The falling ice must have broken them apart. Near the bottom of the iceberg, a prong of ice poked out over the sea like a giant anvil.

When we reversed past the anvil for the third time, I peered carefully beneath it to make sure there were no underwater ice shelves.

Then, on our fourth time round, I gingerly straightened the helm. As the reversing *Black Pimpernel* came out of its sharp right-hand turn, the weight of the ice chunk began to tip us to starboard again. Over we went, further and further, until the waves were splashing through the starboard rails and washing across the deck.

Favouring her sore ankle, Frøya pulled herself up to one of the windows so she could see out.

'Turn, Sam!' she cried. 'We are going to hit that iceberg!'

Captain Dan had dragged himself up, too. He didn't

say anything. I could see him mentally gauging angles and distances and speeds. His face was bathed in sweat.

So was mine. The *Black Pimpernel* was leaning over at an impossible angle – 45 degrees, maybe 50 degrees from the horizontal! At any moment, we were going to capsize.

But still I kept her on a steady course.

Hang in there, ship! I urged her. *Stay upright just a bit longer!*

The *Black Pimpernel* chugged backwards towards the projecting prong of ice. We were nearly there. Thirty metres, 25, 20 . . .

Hang in there! You can do it!

Fifteen metres, ten . . .

Suddenly I felt the floor pitch sideways. The *Black Pimpernel* had passed its point of balance. We were going over!

It takes several seconds for a ship to capsize. Enough time for it to travel quite a long way – even if it's going backwards. I held my breath and watched the ice prong. It loomed above our stern, growing steadily larger as the foundering ship reversed towards it.

Five metres, four metres, three . . .

Here goes nothing! I thought. And spun the helm hard right.

A tremor passed through the *Black Pimpernel*'s hull as its rudder bit into the sea. The ship slewed around in a heart-stopping broadside and fell against the iceberg. Steel met ice with a bone-jarring thump. There was a tortured *SCREEEEECH* as the prong scraped along the side of the bridge, tearing into the superstructure and smashing several of the windows. Then – *CRUNCH!* – the prong collided with the huge block of ice that was sitting on the *Black Pimpernel*'s deck.

The ship shuddered as if it had run into a giant brick wall, and stopped. Almost in slow motion, the massive iceblock rolled into the sea.

Just as I'd hoped.

No longer weighed down by its icy cargo, the *Black Pimpernel* slowly righted herself. Her metal superstructure creaked and groaned. Water poured over the sides into the sea. We'd made it!

Captain Dan turned then and gave me a small nod.

'Nice work,' he said.

17
COMPANY

But our troubles were far from over. The hospital ship was now a lost ship. Not only had the icefall destroyed the *Black Pimpernel*'s radio mast, but it had severed the main electrical cable to the bridge as well. None of the navigational instruments were working, except for a small compass. And that wasn't much help.

'You can't rely on a compass so close to the South Pole,' Captain Dan said. He was slumped in the captain's chair, too weak even to sit up properly. 'Just keep away from icebergs, Sam, until one of the maintenance boys is well enough to fix the wiring.'

Who knew how long that would take? Everyone was

still pretty sick, including Captain Dan. He had to go back below deck after only ten minutes on the bridge. I helped him down to his cabin, then went to check on Harry. My little brother was semiconscious and his teeth were chattering. I made him drink half a mug of water, then found some more blankets and a couple of unused ski jackets to pile on top of him.

'What was that . . . banging noise?' he asked weakly.

'We ran into an iceberg.'

'Wicked!' Harry breathed, and went back to sleep.

I stopped in at the infirmary to get a bandage, then climbed the stairway to the bridge and bound up Frøya's ankle. It was badly swollen and she couldn't walk on it. I helped her to the captain's chair, then took charge of the helm.

I was glad to see that the weather had cleared. There was a good view in all directions. But the only direction that interested me was straight ahead. *Keep away from icebergs*, Captain Dan had said. I didn't need to be told twice. No way was I going within a kilometre of an iceberg after what happened last time.

'We have company,' Frøya said.

I looked where she was pointing, expecting to see another ship, but nothing was there except a few icebergs on the horizon.

'I don't see anyth–'

A spout of vapour shot out of the water about 50 metres to our left. My skin prickled. Harry's and my encounter with the killer whales was still fresh in my mind. Then two more whales spouted in the distance, followed by a third one much closer. Suddenly there was a splash just forward of the *Black Pimpernel*'s bow. A huge glossy mound rolled out of the waves, followed by a broad grey tail. It looked bigger than a killer whale and was so close that I could see barnacles speckled across its rubbery skin.

'Minke whales,' Frøya said, a big smile stretching across her face. 'For sure, they are very beautiful.'

I wouldn't have called them beautiful, but they certainly made an impressive sight. A pod of the huge mammals was swimming across our path from left to right. There must have been a hundred or more.

'Look, there's a little one!' Frøya pointed.

A mother and her half-grown calf had surfaced right next to the ship. The calf was the size of an estate car, but it did look kind of cute. I wished I had a camera.

'They don't seem bothered by us,' I said.

'Why are they to be bothered?' Frøya asked as the mother led her calf around our stern and swam off after the others. 'We are their friends.'

Then I saw something that took my mind off the minke whales. Coming over the horizon to our right was a little black dot. My heart thudded as I grabbed a pair of binoculars from the shelf beneath the radio.

'Helicopter!' I cried. 'It's coming this way.'

'Let me see,' said Frøya, reaching for the binoculars.

She didn't seem very excited about it, but I put that down to her age. She was older than me and trying to be cool. I was too relieved and happy to act cool. I reckon there was a big cheesy grin on my face as I watched the helicopter grow larger and larger. It had come looking for us. Our troubles would soon be over.

'Stinkers!' breathed Frøya.

'What's the matter?'

She passed me back the binoculars. 'Have a look.'

I focused on the approaching helicopter. It wasn't black, it was orange. Painted on its fuselage was a word beginning with **R**. I tried to make out the other letters. There was an **E**, an **S**, another **E**, an **A** . . .

Suddenly I got it: **RESEARCH**.

It was the helicopter I'd seen on the rear deck of the *Nisshin Maru*.

'Are they looking for whales?'

Frøya nodded. 'Already they have found them.'

I watched the helicopter descend and fly in a big circle over the sea about 200 metres to our right, directly above the centre of the pod. Then it rose to about 500 metres and hovered there.

'What are they doing?'

'For sure, they are calling the killer ship,' Frøya said.

I scanned the horizon where the helicopter had first appeared. That's where the whaling fleet would come from. 'What can we do?'

'I don't know.' There were tears of frustration in Frøya's eyes. 'Everyone is sick.'

'Except us,' I said. I pushed the throttle lever all the way forward and spun the big wooden wheel to the right.

18
PLAN B

'What are you doing, Sam?' Frøya asked as the *Black Pimpernel* began to turn slowly towards the helicopter.

'I'm going to chase them away.'

'How can you chase a helicopter?'

'Not the helicopter,' I said. 'The whales.'

My grandparents own a farm in the high country of southern New South Wales. One school holidays, Nan and Pop took me on a cattle round-up. On horses and motorbikes, we rode up into the mountains and drove a big mob of cows down to the winter pastures. I didn't know if whales could be herded up like cows, but it was worth a try.

There were several mother whales with half-grown

calves in the pod, and the whole group was travelling slowly so they wouldn't be left behind. We soon caught up. I turned the *Black Pimpernel* across their path, but instead of changing direction like cattle, the leading whales simply dived underneath us and continued on their way. The rest of the pod swam past behind our stern.

'They will not stop,' Frøya said. 'They are migrating.'

Migrating straight towards the *Nisshin Maru* and the rest of the Japanese whaling fleet.

It was time for Plan B. I turned the wheel the other way and the *Black Pimpernel* slowly came round in a sweeping left-hand turn. When we were travelling parallel with the pod once more, I straightened the helm. Slowly we began overtaking the huge, strung-out line of migrating whales. The helicopter tagged along overhead. The whale spotters must have wondered what we were doing.

'Frøya, can you take the helm?'

'My foot is hurting very much to walk.'

'I'll help you.' I assisted her across to the helm, then propped her injured foot on a rolled-up life jacket. 'Is that OK?'

She nodded and clasped the wheel. I could see she

was in pain, but there was nothing I could do. Someone had to steer the ship while I put Plan B into action.

'Where do they keep the smokebombs?'

Frøya explained how to get to the lazaret, a little storeroom at the rear of the ship. 'You must get the key from Raoul Garcia, the bosun,' she said.

There wasn't time to go searching for Raoul. We were nearly level with the leading whales.

'When we get ahead of the pod,' I called back as I headed for the stairs, 'steer across in front of the whales and slow down.'

Frøya's directions were good. They led me straight to the lazaret. There was a padlock on the door and a sign that said: **Danger, Explosives**.

Excellent! I thought.

Coming along the gangway, I'd passed an axe attached to the wall. It must have been for use in emergencies. This was an emergency. I swung it three times – *Bang! Clang! Chop!* – and the padlock flew apart. The door creaked open.

The smokebombs were in boxes of 12. They weren't heavy, but the bulky cardboard cartons were difficult to handle. One was all I could manage. I lugged it up on deck.

Hooley dooley! I'd forgotten to put on a dry suit and the cold was like an invisible wall. Luckily the rain had passed, but the wind blasted me with pellets of frozen spray. A frosting of ice covered everything. The deck pitched from side to side as the *Black Pimpernel* was tossed about on the heaving sea. I wobbled and slithered towards the stern, keeping away from the edge because half the railing was missing – crushed by our run-in with the iceberg – and I wasn't wearing a life jacket. Not that a life jacket would have been much help if I fell over the side. Even if the Japanese tried to save me in their helicopter, I'd be dead before they got me out of the water.

Suddenly, the *Black Pimpernel* tipped sharply to starboard. Frøya must have turned the ship in front of the whales. She was only doing what I'd asked, but it couldn't have happened at a worse time. My feet went out from under me. I landed on my backside and went sliding across the deck. Straight towards a gap in the railing. The deck was like an ice rink. I couldn't stop.

Shishkebab! I was going to go over the side!

At the very last moment – when I was a metre from the gap in the railing – the ship lurched the other way.

Frøya had seen what was happening and swung the helm hard to port. It was too late to stop my slide, but enough to slow me down. As my feet went over the edge, I arched my body sideways and made a wild grab for one of the davits used for lowering the Zodiacs into the water. My fingers were numb with cold, but somehow they latched around the rusty iron and held on. The Zodiac bobbed in the sea a few metres below my swinging legs, attached by a single rope. The other davit must have snapped when we hit the iceberg. If I'd gone over the side, I might have landed in the Zodiac. Then again, I might have missed it. And been snap-frozen in the icy Antarctic Ocean.

Badly shaken, I pulled myself back on deck and used a ventilator cowl to drag myself upright. The whales were close. They came surging towards the ship in a line that stretched back half a kilometre. Every so often one would break the surface, shooting up a fountain of spray as its ten-tonne body rose out of the sea like a mountain. Sometimes three or four came up at once. A mountain range on the march. They looked unstoppable.

But I had to stop them – or at least make them change course.

Crouched on all fours, I scuttled over to the carton I'd dropped when I fell over. Luckily it hadn't slid overboard. It was jammed under a water cannon. I dragged it clear and ripped it open. Inside, two layers of large green cylinders lay packed side by side like jam jars. They didn't look like bombs. I picked one up and glanced at the long list of instructions written on the side. There wasn't time to read them. A plastic loop on a short string dangled from one end. I gave it a tug.

POP! The top of the cylinder flew off and a plume of bright-orange smoke came billowing out.

Houston, we have ignition!

I hurled the hissing smokebomb at the nearest whale. Missed. It landed in the sea. The whale took no notice. It swam right underneath the bobbing, smoking cylinder as if it wasn't there.

Bummer! This was harder than herding cattle.

I picked up another smokebomb. This time I would get the timing right. I waited until a whale was about to surface, then pulled the loop, took careful aim, and threw.

Bull's-eye!

The smokebomb hit the surfacing whale right on the nose. But the huge creature didn't bat an eyelid. Well, it did – one eye blinked when the cylinder bounced over it – but that was the only reaction I got. The whale kept coming. It swam right up to the *Black Pimpernel*'s stern and disappeared underneath.

I tossed all ten remaining smokebombs at the other whales, but the results were the same. The pod didn't deviate by a single degree. They stayed on course – a course that was going to take them right into the waiting harpoons of the Japanese whaling fleet.

So much for Plan B.

The helicopter circled overhead as I made my way back to the bridge.

'It didn't work,' I said.

Frøya acted as though she hadn't heard me. She didn't even look in my direction. Her eyes were fixed on the horizon ahead and a deep frown etched her forehead.

I turned to see what was so interesting.

Uh oh! Ships. Two of them. Coming straight towards us.

'Are they . . . ?' I asked.

Frøya nodded. 'Rotten stinkers!' she muttered.

19
NO CONTEST

They were still a long way off. Two or three kilometres. But through the binoculars I recognised the familiar square shape of the *Nisshin Maru*. The second ship was smaller. It was low and sleek and looked like a miniature destroyer.

As it came closer, I began to see more details. Instead of cannons, there was a big harpoon gun on the bow. A harpoon designed to kill whales. I'd read about them in *Earth Watch*. The harpoon has an exploding head that goes off inside the whale, causing the huge animal to slowly drown in its own blood. Gross!

'Should I ram them?' I asked. I had taken over the

helm from Frøya, who was back in the captain's chair resting her sore foot.

'For sure, we will all be killed,' she said softly.

I remembered what Captain Dan had said. A fair exchange. But I knew I couldn't do it. The lives of 47 sick people – including Harry – were in my hands. I couldn't jeopardise their safety. Not for all the whales in the world.

But I couldn't just watch as the whales were slaughtered.

Neither could Frøya.

'Sam, see if you can get the *Black Pimpernel* between the whales and the killer ship,' she said.

It was worth a try. The whalers couldn't fire their deadly harpoons if we were in the way. I set the throttle on full speed and put us on a collision course with the killer ship. It was still a long way off. I estimated we had four or five minutes before things got exciting.

'My father is doing this,' Frøya said as the Japanese ships slowly grew larger.

'Stopping whalers?' I asked.

'No. He *is* a whaler. Back in Norway they are still

murdering whales like these Japanese. My father is captain of a whaling ship. That is why I have volunteer for crew on the *Black Pimpernel*.'

'Did you run away from home?'

Frøya sniffed. 'I am 22 years. Old enough to do what I want.'

I had thought she was younger. Closer to my own age. But it didn't matter – I already had a girlfriend. Well, girl *pen*friend. Her name was Michiko Takai and she lived in Japan. I hoped she didn't eat whale meat.

We had caught up with the pod again. I changed course slightly and eased the ship past a mother and her calf. There were whales all around us, swimming on both sides of the *Black Pimpernel* like overgrown dolphins. *Frøya's right*, I thought as one rolled onto its side and slapped a huge fin playfully on the water – *they* are *beautiful*.

Hoot! Hoot! Hoot! The killer ship had drawn ahead of the *Nisshin Maru*. It was 400 metres away and closing fast.

I made a slight adjustment to the helm to avoid a whale, then lined up the Jolly Roger on our bow with the harpoon gun on theirs.

'Which way will they turn?' I asked. My hands were sweaty. I hoped they *were* going to turn.

'Maybe to the right,' Frøya said, sounding nervous. 'Be careful, Sam.'

I *was* being careful – careful not to hit any whales. Most of them were behind us now. But the pod was still swimming in the same direction. Straight towards the approaching vessels. Easy pickings for the Japanese hunters, except for one thing. A black pirate ship that was in the way.

'It is turning,' Frøya said.

She was right. The killer ship's bow began to veer slowly to the right. I spun the *Black Pimpernel*'s wheel.

Hoot! Hoot! Hoot! went their horn, but I didn't flinch. I matched the killer ship's turn. Both vessels were still on a collision course.

I wasn't going to hit them. I was just trying to keep the *Black Pimpernel* between the killer ship and the whales. But the Japanese captain didn't know that. It must have looked like I was going to plough straight into them. With a final, angry *hoooooot!* he chickened out and started to turn away.

'Yessss!' I said, pumping the air with my fist.

It was just like herding cattle.

'Watch out for the other one!' warned Frøya.

I hadn't been watching the other ship. The *Nisshin Maru* had been two or three hundred metres behind the killer ship. When the smaller ship turned, its 8,000-tonne companion turned, too. But not as sharply.

The *Nisshin Maru* seemed to come out of nowhere. Suddenly its huge bow came steamrolling around the killer ship's stern. Straight towards the *Black Pimpernel*. Its captain hadn't seen us, either.

The two ships were going to collide.

It was too late to turn. I slammed the throttle lever into full reverse and braced myself against the wheel as the two ships ploughed towards each other head on. Eight thousand tonnes versus *800* tonnes.

No contest.

20
DIVE, WHALE, DIVE!

The captain of the *Nisshin Maru* must have seen us at the same moment that we saw him. He slammed his ship into reverse as well.

Too late. The two ships came together at an angle, our bow against her side.

SCRE-E-E-E-ECH!

The can opener, the two-metre steel blade on the *Black Pimpernel*'s prow, scraped along the side of the factory ship, leaving a big scratch just below the **MURI** the tagging crew had painted there.

That was the only damage. Both vessels had slowed down to a virtual stall by the time of impact. Then our reversing props bit into the sea and began pulling us away.

As the *Black Pimpernel* reversed out of the factory ship's shadow, a spray of water exploded against the bridge, turning the windows white.

'What's going on?' I gasped.

'They are shooting us with water cannons,' Frøya said, shouting to make herself heard over the roar of water.

I gritted my teeth. I wanted to return their fire – Captain Dan couldn't stop me from using our water cannons now – but I had to stay at the helm. There was nobody else to drive the ship, and we were still perilously close to the *Nisshin Maru*'s towering hull. One wrong move and we'd be crushed like an empty drink can. I reversed until we were 30 or 40 metres away and the water cannons could no longer reach us, then spun the wheel left and pushed the throttle forwards.

'Oh no!' Frøya cried as we emerged from behind the *Nisshin Maru*. Once more we could see the killer ship. It had turned in a huge circle and was coming back towards the whales. 'Stop them, Sam!'

I tried to cut them off, but the *Black Pimpernel* didn't have enough acceleration. We were doing barely four knots when the killer ship surged across our bow at full throttle. A man in orange waterproofs crouched behind the harpoon gun. All we could do was watch as the whale hunters raced towards the pod of unsuspecting minkes.

A whale broke the surface about 100 metres ahead of the killer ship.

'DIVE, WHALE, DIVE!' shrieked Frøya.

It was almost as if the whale heard her. The huge animal started to dive. Its broad fluked tail rose out of the water as the whale rolled forward. But it seemed to be moving in slow motion.

Hurry! I thought, watching the killer ship eat up the distance between them.

The huge tail started sliding back down into the sea. It was going to make it!

There was a puff of smoke from the front of the killer ship and a black steel harpoon shot out across the water. It was almost too fast to see. The whale disappeared. For a moment I thought the harpoon had missed. Then I glimpsed a length of wire running out from the bow of the ship. When the whale went down, the wire snapped taut like a fishing line.

'They got it,' I muttered, feeling sick.

Frøya had jumped out of the captain's chair and hopped over to the window. She peered through the binoculars.

'I do not think the explosion worked,' she said.

I hoped she was right. But what difference would it make in the long run whether the harpoon had exploded or not? The whale still had a harpoon in it. It was still attached to the ship by a strong steel wire. It couldn't escape.

The killer ship was slowing down. Orange-clad figures raced across the forward deck. Thirty metres ahead of the bow, the water boiled like an undersea volcano. A huge tail rose out of the foam and smacked down so hard we heard the bang from the bridge of the *Black Pimpernel*, 200 metres away. Then the whale disappeared again.

But in the brief instant it had been visible, I'd seen the harpoon dangling from one of its tail flukes.

'I was right,' said Frøya. 'The explosion did not work.'

'But the whale can't get away,' I said.

'We can cut the wire with our propeller.'

'Won't it get tangled?'

Frøya shook her head. 'No, Sam. The wire is very thin.

Not like a prop fouler. For sure, our propeller will cut it.'

Hoping she was right, I turned the *Black Pimpernel* across the bow of the killer ship.

The Japanese saw us coming. But there was nothing they could do. The tables were turned – now they were stationary in the water and we were travelling at full speed. The captain began angrily tooting the horn and two of the deckhands aimed a water cannon at us.

I wasn't concerned. My only worry was the whale. It was still underwater somewhere forward of the killer ship's bow. I didn't want to run into it. So I steered the *Black Pimpernel* as close to the Japanese vessel as possible. We passed within a few metres of their bow. The man at the harpoon gun glowered at me over the sights of his weapon as we barged past.

'Stinker!' Frøya shouted at him.

There was a tiny vibration through the floor as the harpoon wire dragged along the underside of the *Black Pimpernel*'s hull. I held my breath, waiting for it to reach the propeller.

Either of two things could happen. The propeller could slice it in two, setting the whale free. Or – if Frøya was wrong and the wire *did* tangle our propeller – the *Black Pimpernel* would be put out of action.

I wondered if the Japanese would help us if our plan backfired. International Maritime Law states that you must assist a stricken vessel at sea, but we were a pirate ship, after all.

I didn't have to worry about it for long.

Twang!

The ship shuddered, the helm gave a tiny twitch . . . and we kept going.

'Look!' Frøya pointed.

Out the port-side window, a huge tail rose into the air. The harpoon was hanging on by a thread. The whale gave its tail a flick and the harpoon came free. It cartwheeled into the sea, trailing three metres of severed wire behind it like the tail of a falling meteor.

Mission accomplished. We'd freed the whale.

But it was just one animal in a pod of about 50. When I looked back at the killer ship, I saw three orange-clad deckhands loading another deadly harpoon into the gun.

21
LOST THE WAR

There's a saying my school basketball coach sometimes uses when we lose a game – we won the battle but lost the war. He means we did really well in one aspect of the game – we had 60 per cent of ball possession, for example – but the other team had too many tall players and they gave us a hiding on the scoreboard.

My basketball coach might have said the same thing if he'd been there when Frøya and I saved the minke whale. We had won a minor battle, but the Japanese were going to win the war. They had too much speed, too much technology, too much firepower, and too many men. No way could a creaky old rust bucket like the *Black*

Pimpernel, crewed by a 14-year-old boy and a girl with a sprained ankle, hope to stop them.

But we could try.

'Go after them,' Frøya cried. 'See if you can get in front.'

I brought the *Black Pimpernel* around in a big, agonisingly slow U-turn and set off after the killer ship. But it was a wasted effort. Already the ship was several hundred metres away, right in among the pod.

I saw a puff of smoke. A whale rolled onto its side. One long fin flapped in the air like the arm of a drowning man.

'No-o-o-o-o-o-o!' Frøya wailed, covering her eyes.

I wanted to cover my eyes, too, but I was in charge of a ship. Grinding my teeth, I steered the *Black Pimpernel* towards the horrific scene. The sea was red with blood. A whale was dying before my eyes.

Frøya and Captain Dan were right: this wasn't research, it was a crime.

I slowed down and brought the *Black Pimpernel* alongside the dying whale. There was nothing I could do. Cutting the harpoon wire wouldn't help it now.

The Japanese deckhands turned their water cannons on us, so I moved further away. Already the *Nisshin Maru* was approaching. The huge factory ship drew up beside the smaller vessel, and a team of workers in orange waterproofs and gumboots lowered cables down its slipway to drag the dead whale aboard for butchering.

'Murderers!' Frøya said.

I silently agreed with her.

22
GAME ON

We left the Japanese to their grisly task. One whale was dead, but the rest of the pod were still alive. We wanted them to stay that way. So we provided the whales with a pirate escort. The *Black Pimpernel* chugged along at the rear of the pod like a big, scruffy watchdog. Frøya and I were its eyes, scanning the ocean in all directions for signs of danger. But mostly we looked behind us, where the two whaling ships sat motionless on the horizon, growing steadily smaller as we sailed away from them. I knew the pod was safe until the Japanese had loaded the dead whale onto the *Nisshin Maru*. Then it would be game on once more.

Except it wasn't a game. More whales were going to die if the killer ship got past us.

Somehow we had to stop it.

'Here they come,' Frøya said.

Both ships had turned in our direction. We had a head start of roughly five kilometres, but it wasn't enough. The whales were swimming at only three or four knots. Much too slow. I'd seen how fast the killer ship could go.

The orange helicopter was the first to arrive. It flew right overhead and circled the whales. I knew the pilot would be in radio contact with the hunters, letting them know the pod's position.

'How far behind are the ships?' I asked, nudging the *Black Pimpernel* right in behind the whales in an effort to make them swim faster.

Frøya had the binoculars. 'About two kilometres.'

'Get a move on, whales!' I muttered under my breath.

But the pod would only swim as fast as the mothers and their calves. And even if they left the young ones behind – which no whale would ever do – they could never outrun the killer ship.

It was time to do something.

'Frøya, can you take the helm?'

'For sure,' she said, hopping over to the wheel on one foot. 'What is it you are doing?'

'I'll try to let out the prop foulers.'

She touched my arm. 'Be careful, Sam.'

I raced down to the stern. This time I didn't even notice the cold. There were more important things on my mind. Like not going backside-down on the slippery deck again and sliding over the side. Like how quickly the killer ship was catching up. Like how to let out the prop foulers without being dragged overboard.

The prop foulers were huge coils of rope, steel cable and plastic floats that had to be unwound and fed carefully over the stern so they didn't tangle. I'd seen the prop-fouler crew doing it a few hours earlier, but there were three of them. Three grown men. There was only one of me, and I was feeling weak from lack of food and from the seasickness that had put me out of action for half our sea journey.

Stop feeling sorry for yourself, said a little voice in my head. *Just get on with it! More whales are going to die if you don't stop the killer ship.*

I found the end of one of the coils. There was rope to begin with, then steel cable – with floats attached at intervals to keep it from sinking. The heavy black rope was sodden with sea water. It felt icy through my gloves. I started dragging it towards the stern. There was a gap to slide it through. Just wide enough for the floats, too narrow for a man. But not too narrow for a 14-year-old boy. I would have to be very careful, or the line might drag me overboard. But first I had to get *it* overboard. It was snagged.

I scrambled back to see what the problem was. Two of the floats were tangled. As I bent to untwist them, I glanced over my shoulder. The killer ship was less than 200 metres away. Water foamed beneath its bow as the sleek, grey vessel ate up the distance between it and the *Black Pimpernel*. It was going to pass us on the left.

What was Frøya *doing*? We had to be in front of the killer ship for the prop foulers to work.

Suddenly the deck tilted sharply as Frøya spun the helm. I should never have doubted her. She'd timed it perfectly. The *Black Pimpernel* turned across the bow of the oncoming ship. It caught the Japanese captain napping. I went skating back to the stern and began feeding the long strand of rope, cable and floats through the gap. It was hard work and my hands were numb with cold, but I didn't stop until the last float splashed into the churning sea below me. Then I stood up and steadied myself against one of the water cannons, waiting to see what would happen. My heart thudded with excitement. The floats went bobbing away astern of the *Black Pimpernel* in a long, curved line. Directly across the path of the killer ship.

If all went to plan, the cable would pass under its hull and tangle in its propellers, putting it out of action.

It didn't work. The Japanese ship was state-of-the-art. It was designed to chase whales, so it had to be super manoeuvrable. As soon as its captain saw the trap we'd laid for him, he turned hard to starboard. The killer ship veered around the line of floats like a giant speedboat, then swung back onto its former course.

Not only had it avoided the prop fouler, it had got around the *Black Pimpernel* as well. We were behind the killer ship now. And the whales were in front.

I raced back up to the bridge. At the top of the stairs, I stopped dead. Frøya was back in the captain's chair. Captain Dan stood at the helm.

'What are you staring at?' he said gruffly. 'You look like you've seen a ghost.'

He did look like a ghost – his face was the right colour – but I didn't dare say that.

'Are you better?' I asked.

'Not much better,' Captain Dan rumbled. There was a bucket on the floor beside him. 'But well enough to get back up here where I belong. You and Frøya did a good job, by the way.'

I looked out the window. The killer ship had almost caught up with the pod. 'But not good enough,' I said.

All we could do was watch as the Japanese hunters moved in on the whales. My teeth were clenched, my hands made fists inside their gloves. At any moment there would be a puff of smoke, then the splash of a huge fin or a tail as another whale went into its death throes.

It didn't happen.

Incredibly, the killer ship broke off its pursuit at the

last moment. It turned almost 90 degrees and began speeding off to the left.

'Look!' Frøya pointed.

Nobody had been watching the helicopter. It had left the pod, too, and was hovering over the sea about a kilometre away.

'Take the helm, bud,' Captain Dan said to me.

He walked to the window and peered through the binoculars in the direction of the helicopter. For a few seconds he didn't move, then I saw his back stiffen.

'Turn hard aport,' he barked over his shoulder. 'Steer straight towards the helicopter.'

'What is it?' Frøya asked.

'Fin whales,' said Captain Dan. 'At least two of them. Get us over there, and don't spare the horses.'

I pushed the throttle lever, but it was already set at full speed. 'We can't go any faster, Captain.'

His shoulders slumped. The killer ship was far ahead of us, halfway to the helicopter already. 'I need a faster ship,' he said through gritted teeth. 'We're no match for the Japanese in this old rust bucket.'

'For sure, a Zodiac is more fast,' Frøya said.

'I can't leave my ship,' said Captain Dan.

'Sam and I will go.'

'You can't walk.'

'It is hands not feet to drive a Zodiac,' said Frøya. 'Sam will help me down the stairs.'

The captain frowned. 'It takes four strong men to launch a Zodiac.'

'There's one already launched,' I said, remembering the one I'd nearly fallen into. 'It's tied to the side of the ship.'

Captain Dan looked at Frøya, then at me.

'Go for it,' he said.

23
GREYHOUNDS
OF THE SEA

I piggybacked Frøya down the stairs, then helped her to the rear deck and over the side into the bouncing Zodiac. A coiled prop fouler took up most of the floor. I was about to jump down next to her when I had a thought.

'Won't be long,' I shouted, and raced back across the deck.

A minute later I returned with a bulky cardboard carton and dropped it on top of the prop fouler. Then I clambered down after it. Frøya already had the outboard motor running.

'Cast off,' she said, and we were away.

I had been in a Zodiac once before – back on the Great

Barrier Reef when some smugglers were after me. That time I'd been running for my life. Now I was involved in another life-and-death race, except this time *I* was doing the chasing. And it wasn't my life that was on the line, it was the lives of some fin whales.

Fin whales can weigh up to 70 tonnes. That's a lot of meat for the Japanese fish markets. No wonder the killer ship had abandoned its pursuit of the minkes to go after them.

It had a big head start – at least half a kilometre – but Frøya had our Zodiac cranked up and we were really moving. Captain Dan couldn't afford to get a new ship, but he hadn't spared the dollars when buying outboard motors for his Zodiacs. It was big, it was powerful, it was fast.

Fin whales are fast, too. They are sometimes called greyhounds of the sea because they are the fastest of the baleen whales. These ones were in a hurry. We could gauge their speed from the helicopter keeping track of them. They were swimming away from the killer ship at about 20 knots. The killer ship was having trouble catching up.

Which gave *us* more time to catch up with the killer ship.

We drew level with it after ten minutes or so. I don't know how fast we were going, but we'd left the *Black Pimpernel* far behind. The *Nisshin Maru* was further back still. Frøya steered the Zodiac wide of the killer ship. Its captain veered in our direction, trying to cut us off. His crew fired water cannons at us, but we were out of range and the white jets of water fell harmlessly into the sea. We bounced over their bow wave and sped away.

I could see one of the whales now. It was about 100 metres ahead. Every few seconds a wide, bluish-grey mound would rise half a metre out of the sea. There would be a spurt of vapour, a flash of dorsal fin, then the huge creature would disappear below the steely grey waves.

Frøya and I were so intent on what was ahead of us that we didn't notice what was *under* us.

Suddenly there was big *bump* and the Zodiac rocked sideways.

Holy guacamole!

A second fin whale rose right beside us. It was humungous – easily 30 metres long. And as wide as a train. Frøya swerved away from it.

Bump!

A third fin whale rose on the other side of us!

The fin whale on our left was only a quarter of the size of the one on our right. They must have been mother and calf. And we were between them. *Not* a good place to be.

'*Look out!*' I yelled.

Frøya was looking the wrong way – at the calf, not the mother – so she didn't see the danger. A tail fluke the size of a Cessna's wing rose out of the water on our right and slapped the outboard motor, spinning us 180 degrees.

Suddenly we were heading back the way we'd come.

Back towards the killer ship. On a collision course!

We were going flat out, the killer ship was going flat out. And the gap was only 50 metres . . . 45 metres . . . 40 . . .

'*TURN!*' I yelled.

Frøya had been knocked off her seat by the whale. She lay in the bottom of the Zodiac, looking dazed and clutching her ankle. The throttle was stuck on maximum revs.

Twenty-five metres . . . 20 metres . . . 15 . . .

I threw myself across the coiled prop fouler and hit the tiller sideways. The Zodiac swerved, tipped, then reared upwards. For a second I thought we'd run into the killer ship and were rolling under its hull, but the only thing we'd run into was her bow wave. It sent us high into the air. I held my breath.

We hit the water with a spine-jarring thump and went speeding away from the Japanese vessel at right angles.

I looked back. The killer ship had turned to avoid us, too, but only by a few degrees. Now it was back on course, and much closer to the whales than we were. I brought the Zodiac around in a big semicircle. I couldn't see the whales, but the helicopter marked their position. It was 100 metres ahead of the Japanese ship, and the killers were closing in. The harpoon gunner stood ready on the bow.

'They're going to kill the mother!' Frøya cried. She was sitting up now, watching with a stunned expression as the killer ship powered towards the whales.

'Can you steer?' I asked.

Frøya nodded and took over the controls.

'Get in front of the killer ship,' I cried. 'Between it and the whales!'

I scrambled into the bow of the Zodiac and ripped

open the cardboard carton. Until now I hadn't noticed the cold – so much had been going on – but my hands felt like blocks of ice as I fumbled to pull out a smokebomb. There was no feeling in my fingers at all. I couldn't grip the little plastic loop. In desperation, I clamped it between my teeth and jerked my head back. *Pop!*

I dropped the hissing smokebomb into the bottom of the Zodiac and pulled another one from the carton.

We got there just in time. The harpoon gunner was taking aim at the mother fin whale when Frøya steered the Zodiac across the killer ship's bow, trailing a wall of orange smoke behind us. I activated another smokebomb and dropped it on the floor plate, near my feet. Now there were four activated smokebombs hissing away in the bottom of the Zodiac. We were a floating smokescreen.

Frøya zigzagged in front of the killer ship so the hunters couldn't see the whales. But I could see them. The mother and her calf were just ahead of us, barely a whale's length away. We were getting closer every moment.

'Slow down!' I said to Frøya.

She was at the back of the Zodiac, completely enveloped in orange smoke. I hoped it wasn't poisonous.

Frøya eased back on the throttle. But she was driving blind and slowed down too much. Suddenly a huge grey shape darkened the orange cloud behind us – the killer ship's bow.

A man's head and shoulders emerged over the top of the smoke. Then the point of a harpoon.

I watched in horror as the harpoon gunner squinted one eye closed and took aim. He could see *over* the smoke cloud. He had a clear shot at the whales. He was going to shoot over our heads.

I thought of the mother whale swimming just ahead of us. How in a few seconds time a steel harpoon the size of a heat-seeking missile would punch through her skin and penetrate several metres into her huge, soft body. Then explode. I thought of the calf swimming beside her. The calf that was about to be orphaned. Was it old enough to fend for itself, or would it suffer a long, slow, miserable death by starvation?

A little voice in my head repeated Captain Dan's words – *a fair exchange, don't you think?*

I stood up.

24
ORCA

The Japanese whale hunter and I were eye to eye. Only 20 metres separated us. We looked at each other across the sights of his harpoon gun. I had a whale's-eye view. The point of the explosive harpoon was aimed right at me.

He waved at me to get out of the way, but I shook my head. I knew he wouldn't shoot. They killed whales, not humans. But if I ducked my head or fell over, he would have a clear shot at the whales.

It was hard to balance. I had one shin braced against the side of the Zodiac, the other against the half-empty carton of smokebombs. But I didn't know how long I could stay upright. The Zodiac was lurching and bumping across the heaving seas as Frøya tried to keep us halfway between the killer ship and the whales. She could see now. One by one the smokebombs were running out of puff. Our smokescreen had all but disappeared.

The killer ship edged closer. Frøya increased our speed slightly and I nearly fell over. I heard the whoosh and gurgle of a whale's breath just ahead of the Zodiac.

The whale hunter shifted his aim to the left. He was going to shoot the baby! I leaned the same way as the harpoon gun. He shook a fist at me in frustration.

I wondered how long Frøya and I could stay between him and the whales. With every second that passed, the killer ship came closer.

We rolled over a particularly large wave and for a second I lost my balance. I bent my knees and steadied myself against the carton, then quickly bobbed up again.

The whale hunter shouted angrily in Japanese and again waved at me to get out of the way.

I took no notice. There was a smokebomb in my hand. I'd grabbed it out of the carton when I nearly fell over. Without taking my eyes off the whale hunter, I lifted it to my mouth, gripped the ring in my teeth, and jerked my head back.

Pop!

I tossed the hissing smokebomb in a big, high arc. It sailed over Frøya's head, across the five metres of water between the Zodiac and the jutting prow of the killer ship, and landed on the deck just in front of the harpoon gun.

Immediately both the whale hunter and his gun disappeared in a cloud of orange smoke.

'Slow down a bit,' I said to Frøya, as I dropped to my hands and knees and scrambled back towards her. 'Take us as close to the bow as you can.'

She nodded and slowed down. She knew without having to be told what I was planning to do. Because of the smokebomb in the bow, the captain couldn't see us from the bridge. And the harpoon gunner couldn't warn him because he couldn't see *anything*.

I grabbed the prop fouler and started dragging it towards the rear of the Zodiac. Frøya leaned sideways to make room for me. But she didn't take her eyes off the towering, knife-like prow of the Japanese ship. We were right underneath it, surfing along on its bow wave. It was a crazy manoeuvre. A moment's lapse in concentration, and the ship would run us down. But Frøya held us in position. She was the daughter of a sea captain and obviously knew all about boats.

My arms quivered as I hauled the end of the prop fouler over the wooden transom next to the outboard motor. I felt weak. Lack of food and the icy conditions had drained nearly all the strength from my muscles. I lowered the first plastic float into the water, then pulled at the heavy coils of rope and cable behind me. They hardly moved.

'Hurry!' Frøya shouted.

I tried again, but my muscles were like jelly. It was maddening. Normally I'm strong. I do weights three times a week and can bench press 40 kilos. But now, when the lives of the mother fin whale and her calf were on the line, I felt as weak as a lamb.

Frøya shouted at me again. She could see I was having trouble and wanted me to take control of the Zodiac so she could have a go. I pretended not to hear her over the roar of the outboard. Avoiding eye contact, I clambered back over the tangled prop fouler and put my back to it. Straining my feet against one of the seats – using my leg muscles, not my jelly-arms – I pushed backwards and up. Slowly the big mound of rope and cable and floats inched up towards the transom.

Then – *splosh!* – it was gone.

Things happened fast. Lying on my back in the bottom of the Zodiac, I saw Frøya pull the outboard hard to the right. The Zodiac spun sideways, zooming out from beneath the bow of the Japanese ship. I heard the outboard scream as Frøya cranked it up to maximum revs.

Twang!

The Zodiac jolted to a sudden stop, sending Frøya crashing on top of me.

The outboard made a whirring sound, then fell silent.

I couldn't see anything. Frøya's shoulder was pressed against my cheek, pinning me down. I was too weak to push her clear.

'Frøya?' I said.

There was an eerie silence. The Zodiac was dead on the water. We rocked over a wave.

'Frøya?' I said, louder this time. 'Are you OK?'

There was a groan. She lifted her shoulder and I caught a glimpse of the edge of the Zodiac and a slice of grey, cloudy sky. 'I have bumped my head very bad,' Frøya whispered.

Suddenly there was another big jolt and she fell back on top of me.

This time I found the strength to wriggle out from under her. Frøya seemed dazed. There was a red mark across her forehead where she had knocked it against the seat. I helped her sit up.

'Oh no!' she gasped, staring past my shoulder.

I turned to see what she was looking at.

Shishkebab! We were right behind the killer ship, almost under its stern.

And it was getting closer every moment.

'They're going to reverse over us!' I cried.

'It is us who are going in the reverse,' Frøya said softly.

'But our motor's stopped!'

Frøya crawled up next to the silent outboard motor and peered down into the water. 'Stinker!' she muttered.

I clambered up next to her. A rope was wrapped around our propeller in a big dark knot. The prop fouler had worked. But not quite the way we'd wanted. I must have pushed it over the rear transom too close to the outboard – it was tangled in *our* propeller!

'But why are we going backwards?' I asked.

Frøya pointed. A line of floats crossed the stretch of dark water between us and the killer ship. Suddenly – *plop!* – the one closest to the ship disappeared.

I realised what was going on. One end of the prop fouler was tangled in our propeller, the other end was tangled in theirs. But their propeller hadn't stopped. One by one, the white plastic floats were being pulled under the Japanese vessel's stern in a boil of frothing water. It was winding us in like a giant fishing reel.

In roughly 30 seconds, we'd be dragged under. No way could we untangle our propeller in time. The knot was huge.

'We have to ditch the outboard!' I cried. It was attached to the transom by two strong steel clamps. 'Is there a shifter on board?'

Frøya gave me a dazed look. She was still groggy from the blow to her head. 'Shifter . . . ?' she said vaguely. 'I do not know this word.'

'It doesn't matter,' I said. Even if I found a shifter, there wasn't enough time to adjust it and undo the clamps. Especially for someone whose fingers felt like blocks of ice.

Another float disappeared. There were only four left. We were really close to the ship. Deep down in the water, the ship's propeller flashed like a giant meat slicer as it reeled us in.

I rose shakily to my feet and started yelling up at the ship: *'HELP! HELP! HELP!'*

Even though we'd been giving the Japanese whalers a hard time, I knew they would rescue us if they saw what was happening.

But nobody appeared at the rail above our heads. They didn't know we were there.

Another float disappeared under the water.

Three to go. And then it would be us.

I turned and looked for the *Black Pimpernel*. It was still half a kilometre away. Too far.

'HE-E-E-E-E-E-ELP!' I screamed, in a final desperate effort to attract the Japanese sailors' attention. But nobody heard me.

We were right underneath the stern now. Only two floats remained on the surface. Two floats between us and a watery grave.

I offered Frøya my hand. 'We have to jump,' I said.

Her fingers closed around mine and I helped her up. Holding hands, we wobbled to the edge of the Zodiac. We both wore life jackets, but drowning wasn't the problem.

After two minutes in the icy water, hypothermia would set in. After five minutes, we'd be dead.

'Good luck, Sam,' Frøya said, and I felt her icy lips on my cheek.

She was kissing me goodbye.

'Good luck, Frøya,' I said, and squeezed her hand.

We turned and faced the water.

The last float disappeared.

'On the count of three,' I said, tensing my legs to jump.

Frøya and I counted together: 'One . . . two . . .'

Before we could say three, a huge black-and-white head burst out of the sea with its mouth wide-open. Frøya and I were knocked over backwards. We landed in a heap in the bottom of the Zodiac.

'Killer whale!' I cried.

'Orca!' cried Frøya.

It saved our lives. It stopped us from jumping overboard and becoming human iceblocks.

At the very last moment, probably when Frøya gave me that goodbye kiss, the prop fouler had done its job. It had broken the Japanese ship's propeller shaft and the huge blades had stopped turning. But we only noticed after the killer whale had come and gone.

'Lucky that killer whale tried to eat us when it did,' I said shakily, as we stared down at the big dark tangle of rope and floats wrapped around the ship's propeller three metres below the surface. 'And not two seconds later.'

'It did not try to eat us,' said Frøya. 'It stopped us from jumping because it knows we will die in the very cold water.'

'But it *wanted* us to die!' I argued. 'They aren't called killer whales for nothing.'

Frøya shook her head. 'They are not any more called killer whales. Now we are calling them orcas. They are part of the family of dolphins.'

I told her about the one that nearly ate Harry and me for breakfast.

'For sure, it was chasing the penguins and the leopard seal,' Frøya said. 'Not you and Harry.'

'You wouldn't say that if you'd been there.'

'I do not have to be there. I know about orcas. They are very smart.'

'Humans are smart, too,' I said. 'I know what I saw.'

'I know what *I* saw two minutes ago,' said Frøya. 'The orca saved us.'

'Only by accident. It was trying to eat us.'

'You are wrong, Sam. Orcas are not dangerous to humans.'

25
WATER CANNON

We were still arguing about it half an hour later on the crowded bridge of the *Black Pimpernel*. Most of the crew had recovered from the food poisoning and stood watching some Japanese seamen in a lifeboat running a heavy cable from the *Nisshin Maru*'s slipway to the bow of the crippled killer ship.

'They will have to tow it all the way back to Japan for repairs,' said Billy.

Captain Dan rubbed his hands together in satisfaction. 'There'll be no more whales killed in Antarctica this season.'

Almost as if they'd heard what Captain Dan was saying,

two fin whales – a mother and her calf – appeared briefly on the surface about 200 metres from the *Black Pimpernel*.

'No more whale meat for the Japanese fish markets,' said Spiro the cook.

Harry, who was sitting in Frøya's lap on the captain's chair, took a big slow breath. 'Please don't talk about food!' he groaned.

Captain Dan laughed. 'That's an order, folks. There'll be no mention of food until we've finished what we came here for.'

'I thought we *were* finished,' said the first officer.

'Not quite. There's just one job left to do,' Captain Dan said mysteriously. 'Take us alongside the *Nisshin Maru*, Billy. Get as close as you can.'

As the *Black Pimpernel* chugged slowly towards the stationary factory ship, Captain Dan turned to the crew. 'Tagging detail, go to your stations. You have some artwork to finish.'

Now I realised what he meant by an unfinished job. Painted on the whaling ship's side in big, dribbly orange letters was: **MURI**. It was time to complete the word.

'Not you,' Captain Dan said to Frøya, who was lifting Harry from her lap and carefully standing up.

'I can do it if someone helps me down the stairs,' she said.

The captain looked at her, then at me. 'Don't just stand there. Give her a hand.'

Two minutes later, we were right alongside the *Nisshin Maru*. This time the massive factory ship couldn't get away because it was tied to the crippled killer ship. I looked on as Frøya and her three helpers completed their message to the world. Where previously there had been the false claim that the *Nisshin Maru* was involved in research, now it would say **MURDERERS**.

It was a condemnation of whaling that would be seen on television and in newspapers right around the planet.

But before Frøya and her team could finish, we heard an approaching outboard motor. The Japanese lifeboat came buzzing alongside. There were six men in the lifeboat and one of them was whirling a grappling hook. They were going to board us and try to stop the tagging crew from completing their message.

There was nobody else on deck – just me, Frøya and her three helpers, and they had a job to do.

'What are you waiting for?' Captain Dan's voice boomed over the loudspeakers. 'Use the water cannon.'

I gave a little salute, 'Aye aye, Captain,' and raced to the nearest cannon.

As I swivelled it towards the port rail, where the first Japanese whaler was about to appear, I caught a glimpse of Harry's face pressed against the window of the bridge above me. Even from 20 metres, I could read the word on his lips.

'Wicked!'